# MY ELUSIVE MATE

## MIDDLEMARCH GATHERING

## SHELLEY MUNRO

**My Elusive Mate**

Print ISBN: 978-1-99-106320-5
Digital ISBN: 978-1-99-106319-9

Editor: Evil Eye Editing

Cover: Kim Killion, The Killion Group, Inc.

Munro Press, New Zealand.

First Munro Press electronic publication March 2023

First Munro Press print publication March 2023

For Paul.

# INTRODUCTION

MARCUS KERR IS A small-town werewolf without a mate. He's not against the idea of a woman in his life, but now that he's older, he's come to accept there mightn't be a mate for him.

Until today.

Now Marcus is confused. He can scent his fated mate, but finding her is another problem.

Ria Hunter is a feline shifter hiding in plain sight. She's an innocent but not so naive that she doesn't understand

1

that danger could swallow her whole if she ever relaxes her guard. A winter storm throws Ria in Marcus's path, but the journey to happy-ever-after is not smooth-sailing for this age-gap pair of lovers. It will take a little seduction and honesty before Ria says yes to the wolf.

# 1

MARCUS KERR JERKED TO an abrupt halt in the middle of a Middlemarch thoroughfare. Agnes Paisley jammed on her brakes and narrowly avoided hitting him. Marcus ignored her shrieks and gestures to inhale deeply, savoring the rich, fragrant scent riding the air. It was a woody, earthy aroma with a hint of smoke and intense chocolate. Hard to describe, but it called his name. He lifted his head, and his nose twitched.

*Yes!* His wolf stirred and attempted to push free of his human body. Claws formed before Marcus grasped his unruly wolf and ceased his shift. *That scent.* He snuffled, prepared to follow the trail until he found the source.

The shriek of brakes and the shove of a vehicle against

his backside yanked him back to the present. He turned to a car horn blast and Valerie McClintock's steely glare. She pushed her spectacles up her nose and wound down her window. "What the devil do you think you're doing, wolf? Only idiots stop on the road. Do you want me to run you over?"

"Sorry," Marcus muttered, scowling at the heat in his cheeks. He normally kept to the background because he was new to Middlemarch. He liked the town and the feline community who'd welcomed him and other members of the Henderson pack after their lives had imploded in Scotland.

"Well, are you moving?" Valerie snapped.

"Yes, of course. I'm sorry for…ah…blocking your way." Marcus retreated and halted on the sidewalk. He waited until Valerie and Agnes drove off before he dragged in another breath. What was that delectable smell? It made his wolf bristle with eagerness. He wanted to burst free and follow that earthy, smoky goodness. Marcus took half a step before his ringing phone stopped him in his tracks. He answered the call. "Yeah."

"Have you bought our coffee yet?" Rory's Scottish burr came down the line.

"No, I'm almost at Storm in a Teacup. Did you want something else?"

"Please. Anita arrived a few minutes ago. Could you get her a coffee?"

"No problem," Marcus said. "Be back in ten." He could follow the scent trail for a bit since it was in the café's direction. He drew the luscious fragrance deep into his lungs. It was like a drug to his wolf, and to be honest, Marcus found himself intoxicated, too.

But what was it?

*Mate*, his wolf supplied, the gruff thought echoing through Marcus's mind.

Shock had him freezing on the footpath. He turned the idea over in his mind and rejected it.

*Mate*, his wolf repeated, this time with a trace of impatience.

Aware of the passing time, Marcus set off at a jog and, on reaching the café, he pushed inside.

The café was busy. He joined the end of the line, waving at the wolves and newer acquaintances he'd made since arriving in the country town.

"Hi, Marcus," Emily, the café owner, said. "I haven't seen you for a while. I hear you and Rory scored a big job

5

making furniture for Lanark Castle."

Marcus smiled. "The Middlemarch grapevine is efficient."

"Yes, it is. We pride ourselves on our economy of speed. What would you like today?"

"Five flat whites, please. To go."

Emily scribbled the order and slapped the slip on a spike for Tomasine, her employee. Marcus handed over his credit card, and after paying, stepped aside to let the next person place their order.

His next breath contained more of the scent, tinged with coffee and melted cheese. More alert, he scanned the cafe's occupants. He spotted the same wolves, felines, and humans he'd seen during his first quick perusal, yet with every breath he took, he became more aware of the attention-grabbing fragrance.

"Marcus, your coffees are ready," Tomasine called.

Marcus shook himself from his trance and strode to the counter to collect the coffee. "Thanks, Tomasine."

His mind, or rather his nose, was playing tricks on him. Marcus headed for the door, coffee in hand. He'd come back later this evening, maybe when it was dark, and try to locate the scent trail.

In his peripheral vision, he spotted a café patron—an elderly woman. She hunched forward, the tap-tap-tap of her walking stick loud on the wooden floor. Marcus used his free hand to open the door for her.

"Thank you, son," she said in a high, creaky voice that sounded as if it got little use. She teetered past him, ambling along the path and around the corner.

Marcus stood stock-still, his brain whirling with disbelief.

*Mate,* his wolf moaned.

He cautiously stepped outside and allowed the door to close. He sniffed and scowled. Bloody hell. He was losing his marbles.

*Mate.*

Marcus snorted. They were off their rocker. No way in hell was that old woman their mate, no matter how enticing her scent.

# 2

RAIN SPLATTERED FROM SULLEN gray clouds, as it had done for the last two days. Marcus and his best friend Rory splashed through shallow puddles and skirted the deeper ones on their way to the Middlemarch town hall. Sturdy vehicles filled the car park, and dozens of men dressed in boots and heavy-weather gear stood in groups. There was chatter, but overall, a solemn air hovered over everyone.

The Mitchell brothers—all feline shifters—arrived next, along with Isabella Mitchell. Saber, the oldest brother and the Feline Council leader, didn't waste time. Marcus and Rory joined several of their fellow wolf shifters.

"We'll split into groups and check the outlying homes. The river is high, and several roads are underwater.

The ladies will arrange beds for those who must leave their homes. We'll set up emergency housing here in the hall. If you need to help residents evacuate their homes, remember lives are more important than possessions. Just bring the necessities. Make sure pets are safe. The next two days will see more of this wild weather."

A deafening thunderclap boomed overhead, and Saber paused. The bright white of an electrical flash showed through the window as a lightning bolt crackled through the sky.

Marcus lived in a rental property set on a hillside. While he was confident it would remain clear of the flood waters, he worried one of the surrounding trees might end up in his living room.

Saber started talking again before assigning groups to visit specific homes. As soon as the men received their task, they moved out in pairs.

"Marcus, Rory, I want you to check on the Taylors. Their home is on the riverbank, so I'm picking they'll need to evacuate here to the hall. You'll need two vehicles because they have six children." Saber gave them quick directions to make sure they understood where to go. "Questions?"

"No," Marcus said. "We'll return as soon as we can."

Their trip back to their vehicles was miserable and done at speed since the rain was worse than earlier. The wind howled along the main street, almost tearing off Marcus's hat. He gripped the peak and held it in position while trying to ignore the creep of chilly water beneath his coat collar.

While he and Rory hadn't lived in Middlemarch for long, he didn't complain about the pouring rain or the chill in the air. Nor did he whine that he'd rather be at home. The community of Middlemarch had welcomed their bedraggled pack, giving them a fresh start. Helping during a crisis was a tiny repayment.

Marcus started his vehicle and put the windshield wipers at full speed. Even then, visibility was poor, and he crawled toward the river. When they arrived at the Taylor house, the water was up to the second step, almost forcing its way into the squat one-level home. The house lay in darkness, but Mrs. Taylor was scurrying back and forth with towels to place in front of the door. Marcus didn't think it would help.

"Is your husband here?" Rory asked, wading through the rainwater and coming to a halt by Marcus.

"No, he had a load to deliver in Christchurch. He won't return until tomorrow." Mrs. Taylor bore a pale face with deep shadows beneath her eyes. Her children hovered behind her, their expressions equally anxious.

"The rain is getting worse," Rory said.

Mrs. Taylor blinked hard several times.

Marcus spoke up. "You should come with us. We'll take you to the town hall. You can at least have a hot meal and a dry place to sleep."

She hesitated before glancing at the churning, roaring river. Tree branches and other debris swept past in the furious muddy-brown current. Mrs. Taylor swallowed audibly. "Is there room for everyone?"

"We have two vehicles," Rory said. "Why don't we get started? Grab warm clothes and put on your coats and hats."

"What about Tabitha?" a tiny blonde girl cried.

"Tabitha?" Marcus asked.

"Our cat," Mrs. Taylor replied.

"Do you have a cat cage?" Marcus asked.

"Yes, but she hates it. It's a monumental job to get her in it."

Marcus and Rory exchanged a glance.

Marcus forced a smile and focused on the little girl. "We'll make sure Tabitha comes with us. Do you have food for her?"

"I'll organize it," Mrs. Taylor said, happier now that she'd decided to leave.

Rory and Marcus swung into action, helping the younger ones to don warm clothing and coats while Mrs. Taylor packed clothes. Once they'd finished, he and Rory took a child each and piggy-backed them through the water. They loaded them into Rory's vehicle at the rear and returned for two more children.

Rory left with the four kids and their belongings. When Marcus returned from his second trip, the little girl was crying, and Mrs. Taylor wasn't far from weeping, either. "The cat?" he asked.

Mrs. Taylor lifted her right hand. Nasty scratches bloomed blood on her forearm.

"Where is it?"

"I trapped Tabitha in the bedroom to the right, but I couldn't catch her."

"You get your stuff and wait in my vehicle. I won't be long."

Ten minutes later, Marcus strode outside with the

snarling cat locked inside her carry cage. Mrs. Taylor goggled at his scratched face and arms and started apologizing.

"It's all right," he said, although inwardly, he cursed the feline. He got she was frightened and had sensed his wolf, but he was trying to save the wretched animal. "We have the cat." In the short time he and Rory had been here, the water had risen farther, and it now lapped at the top step.

It was a slow drive to town. The rain was still torrential, and visibility was poor. His truck slipped and slid on the slick road, and Mrs. Taylor pressed her hands against the dash, a hiss escaping her. When Marcus finally pulled up at the town hall, she relaxed.

"Thank you," she said. "I don't know what I would've done if you hadn't come to help." She glanced at the scratches on his cheek and winced. "Thanks for everything."

"You're welcome." He helped her carry her bags into the hall before searching for Saber and Rory. He found the two men together.

"What happened to you?" Rory asked.

Marcus scowled at the rapidly healing scratches on his hands. "Mrs. Taylor's cat. We had a difference of opinion."

Rory made a tsking sound while Saber grinned.

"Go home," Saber said to Rory. "We've done what we can, although if the rain continues, I'm worried the town will flood. I'd prefer if you were at home with your families." He consulted his list. "Marcus, would you mind dropping in to see old Mrs. Hunter? She's a wily old bird and self-sufficient, but I'd rest better if someone checked on her. It won't take you much out of your way. She lives on Rata Road, which isn't far from you. Look for a bright red mailbox on the right-hand side of the road. She lives at the end of a long drive."

Marcus's wolf stirred.

*Mate.*

"Sure, I'll do it now," Marcus said, ignoring his wolf. The woman was old, stooped, and probably twice his age, given her wizened face. "Call if you need help with anything. You too, Rory."

"Our place should be out of harm's way, but I'd prefer to get home. The water is rising fast," Rory said.

"Go. Both of you," Saber said. "Valerie and Agnes have everything in hand. I'd like to go home to Emily and the girls."

Rory and Marcus headed out together and parted ways

at their vehicles. It was dark now, and most residents would hunker down in their homes and hopefully stay safe from the floodwaters. Marcus pulled out and drove toward home. While he loved Middlemarch life—more peaceful after living with Elizabeth Henderson throwing her weight around—he found himself lonely. Building furniture helped to fill the empty hours, as did doing repairs to his house, but he couldn't help feeling envious of Rory, who'd found Anita. The other couples in Middlemarch were close, and seeing happy couples—mates—in every direction didn't help to squelch his envy.

Deep in thought, he almost missed the turnoff to Rata Road. He stopped and backed up to take the left-hand turn onto the gravel surface. It was more like a fast-racing stream than a road, and his tires struggled to gain traction. He changed down a gear and muscled his way through the mud and water.

A jagged lightning bolt lit his surroundings, and he spotted the red mailbox by luck. Seconds later, a thunderclap sounded directly overhead. Marcus winced and brought his vehicle to a standstill as his headlights illuminated what looked like a lake. He wouldn't be driving this road. He hesitated because Saber had said Mrs. Hunter was a capable woman. Then his shoulders slumped. He'd never forgive himself if something happened because he hadn't checked on her.

Decision made, he parked on the highest spot he could find and hoped the floodwater wouldn't do any damage before his return. He reached over into the rear seat to grab his heavy raincoat. Water spilled over the top of his gumboots a mere four steps from the truck, and he cursed under his breath. Old Mrs. Hunter was a pain in his backside.

*Mate*, his wolf supplied.

"Not helpful," Marcus ground out. He couldn't even be confident the scent had come from her. What if she'd come into contact with the true owner of the fragrance? But Mrs. Hunter might answer his questions if he asked because there was something about the mystery fragrance that had spiked need and want in him and his wolf.

Marcus splashed through the water. In the distance, he spotted lights. Reports had come in that the electricity was out in parts of Middlemarch, so she was lucky. At the very least, he might get a hot drink upon arrival.

# 3

RIA LISTENED TO THE thump of the rain on the roof. Outside, bolts of lightning streaked across the night sky. Thumber boomed overhead, and she swore ozone filled the air, which was not great. The strikes were too close. The wind howled like a mythical banshee, and the trees rattled and creaked, leaves and small branches flying. Now and then, the scratchy thunk of branches striking her roof added to the cacophony of the storm soundtrack.

Uneasiness skittered down her spine, and she jumped to her feet and stalked to her tiny kitchen. She filled her kettle and put it on to boil, part of her surprised the power hadn't failed. She'd feel better if she could fill her thermos.

In almost two years of living in Middlemarch, she hadn't

suffered through a storm like this. The tiny hairs on her neck bristled, and her ears pricked as she struggled to hear every sound.

"It's just the storm," she whispered. "It will pass."

Edginess forced her to move, and she stalked a circuit of her house, checking every room and inspecting the roof and windows for signs of water leakage. Her cottage sat on the side of a hill, and trees surrounded it, which gave the building shelter, but still, uneasiness filled her. Her tail swished beneath her full skirt as she returned to the kitchen, her slippers scuffing against the cream floor tiles. The kettle switched off as she entered the room, and she poured the boiling water into her thermos and tightened the cap before setting it aside.

Perhaps a cup of tea would settle her nerves. She grabbed a coffee mug and plunked a tea bag inside it. Soon, a piquant mint fragrance rose, and she inhaled, savoring the invigorating scent.

Lightning flashed, the bright light illuminating the valley and the distant river. In that glance, she noted the raging water had escaped the channel and flowed into the paddocks. A massive boom had her jumping, and apprehension crawled across her skin. That had been close.

Lightning flickered almost instantly, a pungent chemical stench filling the air. Another bolt came, seconds after the first, the crack of thunder on its heels. The world seemed to pause, to take a breath, then the entire house shifted, shoving her off-balance.

Hot tea spilled on her wrist, and she dropped her cup as she struggled to stay on her feet. The floor moved and jerked to a stop, throwing her off-kilter again. She couldn't save herself and fell, striking her head on the countertop as she tumbled. Pain sliced through her, stealing her breath, and blackness closed over her.

MARCUS SLOGGED THROUGH THE water, and the icy liquid that sloshed over his boots chilled his feet to the bone. Overhead, lightning forks blasted across the black sky, beautiful but deadly. The accompanying thunder had his blood pumping and his wolf whining. Marcus didn't like this much, but he had to confirm the old woman's safety. His conscience wouldn't allow him to retreat and drive home without knowing she was safe.

A flash of lightning showed him glimpses of the cottage perched on the side of the hill. The tempest sat directly above, and rain lashed him, finding its way through his coat and soaking his clothes. Like his wolf, he hated this storm. A nasty chlorine bleach odor filled each breath, and he increased his speed.

Another whip of lightning forked across the sky, striking a tree. A boom of thunder drowned out the crack as a branch crashed to the ground, taking other limbs with the force of its fall. More lightning. Thunder. Then a breath of silence before an ominous rushing sound. Marcus froze, cocking his head. Then his surroundings brightened with lightning, and horror swamped him.

*Landslide!*

He heard the roar and surge of earth. The slide of mud and rocks. The crash of toppled trees. A second burst of bright light showed him the house, and it was gliding down the hill. It moved slowly at first before gathering momentum. The building crashed into a gigantic tree with a girth twice his size. A loud screech rent the air, the collision of timber against timber. A mountain of dirt and mud flowed after the dwelling. Then the lightning faded, leaving pitch black darkness.

Marcus cast out his senses. Was old Mrs. Hunter even there? If she was sensible, she might've joined a friend.

He pictured the woman and rethought. No, Saber had told him she was independent. He peered through the gloom and picked his way through the debris and deep puddles of water and mud. When he reached the house, he discovered it lodged against two massive trees. The trees seemed deep-rooted, and so far, they kept the cottage in place and stopped it from sweeping farther down the hill. But how long would they hold?

A tree blocked the front entrance, so Marcus skirted the building and slipped around the back. The storm hovered overhead, with regular lightning flashes brightening the murky sky. His clothes clung to his clammy skin with each step as he leaned into the forceful wind. No rear entrance. Strange, but the cottage wasn't large. He checked the windows and found one cracked open. He applied his weight, and the frame squeaked a protest as it moved inward.

Marcus called out. "Hello? Anyone there?" He cocked his head, listening, but heard nothing above the wail of the wind, the whip of lightning, and the clap of thunder.

He hesitated before deciding he'd prefer an elderly lady cranky at him for breaking into her home rather than failing to help someone in need. And—he and his wolf both brightened—they might gain a clue as to the owner of that beautiful, decadent scent.

*Mate*, his wolf growled.

Marcus didn't respond but shoved at the window until it gave with a grumpy squeak.

"Hello," he shouted.

Still nothing.

He continued pushing and scowled when the latch would move no further. It was gonna be a tight squeeze, and he'd end up forcing or breaking the mechanism to get inside. The frame gave way with a crack, thankfully drowned out by a timely boom of thunder. Marcus shoved through the resulting gap and found himself in a laundry. At the doorway, he glanced at his boots and winced at the mud trail. Frowning, he slipped his feet free and then rolled off his socks, as they were as muddy and wet as his outer footwear. One further step into the kitchen, and he froze in position, every one of his senses alerted.

That scent.

It was everywhere.

It filled his lungs, and his wolf's growl rumbled through him, low and husky and full of need.

Marcus swallowed because his mouth had turned dry

as an arid desert. Was his mate someone who was living with old Mrs. Hunter? And heck! He had to stop thinking of her as old. While it was true, he'd hate to blurt it out if his mind went blank. With tension writhing through his muscles, he started a systematic search of the cottage interior. The earthy smokiness filled each room and had an unwelcome side effect. Thank Hades his coat was a long one and hid many sins. He scanned the homey lounge, which was tidy, although a few books lay on the floor along with a smashed vase. Probably had happened when the house had slid off its foundation. Nothing in the first bedroom he checked. He moved onward, down the passage where the enticing scent was more potent.

Marcus paused in the kitchen doorway and cursed under his breath when he spotted a still form. It wasn't the old woman since this person wore a skirt that had rucked up to display shapely limbs.

The entire house shuddered without warning, and Marcus took two giant steps toward the still woman. He crouched, searching for a pulse. He didn't like how the house was moving and needed to get them out before the building surged down the hillside.

A pulse beat beneath his fingertip. At least the woman

was still alive. He leaned closer and caught the scent of blood along with the more enticing one that had first captured his attention. A feline shifter, his brain supplied. It was simple to find the blood source—a wound on the back of her skull. She must've struck her head when she'd fallen.

He checked for broken bones before carefully turning her onto her back.

The house jerked, and something crashed against an outside wall, making the floor shudder. That was it. They had to leave before the enormous trees gave way.

Marcus searched for something to cover her and keep at least some of the rain off. Another thought occurred, and he checked the front door. If possible, it'd be easier to exit that way rather than squeeze the woman through the window.

He gingerly opened the door and searched the darkness. Yes, he thought he could get them out this way, but he'd need to hurry. If only it weren't so dark. Even with his excellent night vision, it was going to be a case of blundering in the gloom.

Marcus grabbed his footwear and pulled on his socks and boots before hustling back to the woman. He found her as he'd left her. Damn, moving her wasn't a great idea, but he couldn't leave her here either. And where the hell was the old woman? He had found no sign of her—just this unconscious mystery woman.

Another tremor of the floor beneath his feet had him bursting into action. He wrapped a blanket around the woman's head and shoulders, then scooped her up and headed for the door.

Damn. The slight shift had shrunk the gap at the front door. Marcus squeezed through, scraping his back as he attempted to maneuver the woman without hurting her. He was almost out when the doorway jerked, and the entire building slid sideways. One tree let out a protesting squeal, and the slide didn't halt. Without hesitation, Marcus jumped. He landed awkwardly, twisting his ankle in an unseen, water-filled hole. Pain shot up his leg, but the wrenching and groaning sounds from the trees and the house had him sucking up his agony.

A jagged snap had Marcus whirling, and he watched with horror as the tree gave way. The second tree fell with a muffled crash, and the cottage slid farther down the hill, gradually gaining speed until darkness engulfed it.

Hell, if he'd hesitated even seconds longer, he and the

woman would've gone over the edge with the house.

# 4

MARCUS TRUDGED DOWN A muddy track, slipping, sliding, and splashing through deep puddles. The wind hurled leaves and tiny branches, and one struck him on the cheek. The sharp gouge told him the twig had drawn blood. But as uncomfortable as he was in his sodden clothes and with his throbbing ankle and cheek, contentment spread through him. He carried his mate in his arms.

Hell, he hadn't even gotten a decent look at her. She was unconscious, but she was breathing. That she hadn't woken worried him, but he could take her to Gavin, the local shifter doctor.

With his ankle, it took him longer to reach his vehicle.

The storm had moved on, but lightning still filled the sky with enough brightness to play havoc with his vision. Rain continued to fall, and the water underfoot had risen. That concerned him too, and he hoped his truck would make it back to town.

The woman didn't stir when he placed her in his passenger seat. As soon as he slid behind the wheel, he started his vehicle, relieved when the engine turned over easily. He put the heater on full blast and set the truck in gear. He drove slowly, carefully, gauging the road's location from the markers on the shoulder. Confidence filled him once he reached the main road until he approached a bridge that crossed a stream. The previous tiny trickle was now a raging torrent, and if the bridge was there, he couldn't see it.

"Damn," he muttered.

He stared at the spot where the crossing used to be for a fraction longer before backing until he could turn his vehicle. He'd be heading for his house until they could get to town. Hopefully, the phones were still working.

He drove equally slowly toward his home, and his ankle protested the entire way. A shiver racked his body, his numerous aches and pains and the cold giving his wolf half a challenge. If something had happened to his rental, he wasn't sure what he'd do.

His headlights slashed the darkness, piercing the rain and giving him a little visibility. The woman's scent filled each inhalation, and he wished he could see her in the light. He peeked at her before returning his focus to the slick road. He'd gained an impression of long limbs, long hair, and not much else.

It had been so dark in that cottage he had seen little of her face, but her skin and hair had been soft beneath his touch. So soft. And he didn't have time to daydream about sex with this woman or anything else. His mission was to get her to safety and to tend her until she regained consciousness.

Marcus gripped the steering wheel tighter and concentrated on driving. The short ten-minute drive took him over half an hour, and tension still filled him when he guided his truck up his driveway. The tires spun for purchase, and he dropped a gear. His vehicle slid, almost going over the bank before he righted the direction, and his knuckles were white by the time he pulled up in front of his house.

A glance told him apart from a fallen tree, which

looked as if it had totaled the garage, his home had survived the worst of the storm. He parked his truck and double-checked the handbrake. The puddles and flying debris were just as bad here, and Marcus stepped into water that was deeper than his boots were tall before he reached his door. He never locked it, and he pushed it open and used the doorstop to keep it from slamming shut.

The woman sat silently in the passenger seat, draped in the blanket and unmoving. Not a great sign. Worry filled Marcus as he awkwardly carried her inside. With the door shut, the wail of blustery wind and the patter of rain lessened. He toed off his gumboots and walked into his bedroom. After placing her on the bed, he shucked his damp socks and switched on the heat pump before turning his attention back to his guest. He couldn't see much of her—just the top of her head. The blanket was wet and probably her clothes, too. He hesitated to strip her yet couldn't think of an alternative. It wasn't as if he intended to take advantage of her. All he wanted was to make her comfortable and warm before he attempted to ask Gavin for advice.

Marcus edged closer to the bed and unfurled the wet blanket. Her long hair was a strange mixture of blonde and dark, with strands of gold. She bore a decent-sized lump on her head, and her hair was red with blood around the wound. The bleeding seemed to have stopped, her shifter status helping her to heal even though she wasn't conscious. He thought she'd be all right, given her breathing seemed normal.

Her clothes clung to her curves, and her skin was icy cold. Marcus hesitated. She could tell him off later. Right now, he needed to get her warm. One of his T-shirts would do. Marcus grabbed a tee first, then unbuttoned her shirt and her undergarments. Next came her skirt.

Her scent told him she was a feline. Now that he had more light, he turned her over, and his breath caught. He blinked, but his eyes were not playing tricks on him. He stared, shook himself, and decided he'd worry about her differences later. Her breathing was still even, so he knew she was alive. This... She... Hell, he had more questions now than when he'd found her.

Powerless to stop himself, he stroked the orange and black fur—to ensure it was real and his mind wasn't playing tricks on him. She moaned, and he froze, his gaze going to her face. Holy crap! How had he not noticed earlier? Her thick, multi-colored strands of hair had shifted and parted to reveal triangle ears.

Marcus shook himself and maneuvered the T-shirt over her head. Once he'd covered her body, he tugged aside the covers and placed her in his bed.

He gathered the wet clothes and the blanket and took them to his small laundry area. They smelled of her, and the smoky scent soothed the angst that had surfaced in him. One thing was for sure. He didn't understand.

His mate...

He shook his head. Once he'd dumped the wet items in the tub, he returned to his bedroom and grabbed dry clothes for himself. That done, he retreated, closing the door behind him. He showered to wash off the mud and blood—thankfully, his wounds had mostly healed—changed into the clean, dry apparel, and placed his laundry with the woman's.

First, he needed to contact Gavin. It was still raining, although not as heavily as earlier, and the thunderstorm no longer hovered over Middlemarch. He hit speed-dial and waited. The phone crackled, and the ringing stopped without warning. He thought he heard a voice, but before he could speak, the line went dead. Marcus tried again, and this time, it didn't even ring.

He gave up and heated soup. Anita had given him some the previous day, and he figured if the woman roused, something warm to fill her belly couldn't hurt. He'd feel better if she regained consciousness.

*Mate*, his wolf said, his growly possessiveness clear.

Marcus agreed, but this woman was an original. She was beautiful with her unusual three-tone hair and her body—he'd tried not to stare when he'd undressed her, but so help him, he was a red-blooded male, and this was his mate, but she was dangerously diverse. That was a concern.

# 5

Ria bolted upright, her heart banging against her breastbone and every iota of self-protection screaming danger. Her nose twitched as she attempted to catalog scents.

*Wrong scents.*

Not her home.

Information pelted her, yet not a bit made sense. Her ears pricked, and sounds assaulted her. Intelligible sounds instead of the usual muted ones. She lifted her chin, eyes scanning, scanning, scanning, and trying to gather facts. The hair raised at her nape, and her tail twitched, betraying her agitation. She swallowed hard, freezing in indecision.

Danger. Danger. *Danger!*

She sprang upward and whirled, bumping into a piece of furniture. Something crashed to the ground, and rapid footsteps headed her way. The door flew open, and a huge, dark form stood in the doorway.

No! No, she couldn't suffer that again. She'd sooner die than face a life of imprisonment. Experimentation.

She growled, the sound not as threatening as she wanted.

"It's all right," a masculine voice said. "I don't wish to hurt you."

She blinked rapidly, and her tail thudded the hard surface she currently cowered against. Her hands prickled, and her claws descended, protruding beneath her fingernails.

"You hit your head."

She frowned, not recalling that, but she remembered the fierce storm—the thunder and lightning and how her house had rattled under the force of nature. Warily, she watched the large man. Her nostrils flared as she dragged in a breath.

*Wolf.*

She swallowed. "Where am I?" This place wasn't a lab. This man... This wolf... A quick shake of her head didn't clear her fuzziness, and a jolt of pain stabbed at her skull.

Her balance wavered, and suddenly the man was closer. Something about his scent struck her as familiar. It was pleasant, with a fresh green, piney tang.

He observed her closely, just like the scientists. She couldn't decipher his expression, and he'd arranged his features in a severe mien that she didn't, couldn't trust. She backed away, ruing the hardwood at her spine. He'd trapped her in a corner, and she hated how vulnerable this made her feel.

"Please, I don't want to hurt you. You're at my house. I didn't know where else to take you because the water has swept away the bridge over the stream. Your house—" He broke off and moved closer still.

"Stay away." She hated the apprehensive note in her voice. The clear tremor that broadcasted her fear when she needed to show strength.

He raised his hands in the air, and they were empty. No weapons. The thought allowed her to relax, but he was bigger than her. He could overpower her. No! No, she refused to let that happen. Never going back. Die first. She wobbled and slapped a hand on the nearest surface to maintain her upright stance.

"You're hurt," he said in his husky voice. "Please sit

down. I promise I have no desire to hurt you."

Somewhere in the distance, a phone rang.

"Oh, good. The phone is working again."

He retreated, and panic roared through her. No! She couldn't let him answer that call. They were alone, which meant she had a chance to escape. If other people came, that would be the end for her. They'd lock her up and never release her. They wouldn't be stupid enough to let her escape twice. She'd die in that place, and no one would care. Certainly not her traitorous brother, her one remaining family member.

These thoughts, aided by memories, flashed through her mind in fleeting seconds. The man turned his back on her, and she sprang. She struck him cleanly and took him to the ground. Her claws dug into his muscular arms when he tried to move.

"Hey!" he complained. "If you want me that badly, just ask."

Confusion pounded her foggy mind before clarity came. Oh!

Somewhere in another room, the ringing started again.

"Let me answer the phone. That's probably Saber wanting to know if I caught up with old Mrs. Hunter.

He wanted to make sure she was safe from the storm."
He struggled to escape her, and she let him wriggle free
this time. The wolf scrambled to his feet and scowled at
her, eyes golden orbs of irritation. He disappeared, and the
ringing ceased.

"Damn and blast," he shouted.

Ria picked herself off the floor and sat on the edge of
the bed, thoroughly confused. Before she could force her
aching head to focus and help her sort out what to do with
this wolf, he'd returned.

"The phone is not working. I've texted Saber to tell him
Mrs. Hunter wasn't at home and must've hunkered down
elsewhere. Hopefully, the text will get through. Do you
know where she is?"

Ria stared and didn't reply.

He halted, his scrutiny intense. That was when she
realized she was wearing nothing but a long T-shirt. No
underwear. No long, full skirt to hide her tail. His gaze
swept her body, pausing where her tail protruded beneath
the gray fabric. After a protracted moment, his eyes lifted.
He did a visual sweep upward, dallying at her breasts
before resting on her hair and finally settling on her ears.

Heat seared her cheeks, but she remained silent. He

wasn't trying to hurt her, and Saber was the leader of the Feline Council. Sending residents out to check on others sounded plausible. It was something Saber Mitchell would do. He'd organized a local to cut wood to feed her fire over the winter. It had been a small gesture and a welcome one, even though she'd told Saber not to repeat the exercise. She might be old, but she wasn't helpless, and she'd cut her wood.

The light was better out here, or maybe it was dawn because she could see his face. He was big—tall—without being bulky and older than her, yet the wolf had muscles that made her a little breathless if she were honest. His brown hair was sticking up as if he'd run his fingers through it a dozen times.

"Are you hungry?"

Ria was glad of the subject change, but suspicion leaped to the fore. What if this was a ruse? What if he'd done his research and, given he was a shifter, knew about Saber? "Food?" she asked, not bothering to hide her distrust.

A frown formed on his brow, and his eyes rolled upward. His quick sniff of annoyance amused her, but she didn't make the mistake of smiling. Now wasn't the time to relax when she had no idea where she was or what he intended to do with her.

"I have soup," he said. "I'll heat it and make toast." Without waiting for a reply, he stalked away.

She started to follow before deciding she'd prefer to don more garments. She fled to the bedroom where she'd woken and searched for her clothes. They were nowhere to be found, and stymied, she placed her hands on her hips. In the distance, the clunk of a pot sounded, so he was making food. Of course, she wouldn't eat unless he did, but if this was a trick, he was a skilled operative. When she couldn't find her apparel, she opened the drawers and the wardrobe. Ah! A pair of track pants. She took them from the drawer and pulled them on. They were too big, but she turned over the waistband and the legs before doing an experimental jump. Yes, they'd remain in place without a belt. In another drawer, she discovered an oversized black sweatshirt. She pulled that over her head, immediately feeling warmer and more in control. The scent coming from the clothes brought a jolt of happiness. They smelled like that man, but she didn't dwell on this, not wanting to unpack what it might mean. The scientists were a tricky bunch and capable of surprising her.

Her house had moved.

The thought slid into her brain, and she snatched it tight. Yes, the entire building had lurched and sent her flying. She lifted her hand and prodded a tender spot. Where had the man found her? In her home? Even more importantly, she needed to ask questions.

She raised her chin and followed her nose. The man had his back to her when she entered the small kitchen, but he must've heard her arrive because he turned to face her, a wooden spoon in hand. His brows rose and one corner of his mouth lifted in a half grin. His intoxicating scent and apparent happiness had her almost returning the sentiment. She froze the twitch of her mouth before it widened to a smile. No, she shouldn't encourage this man. She'd seen him in town and recognized the danger he posed to her, so she'd kept her distance and ignored him.

"Please," he said, his gaze doing a quick up and down of her body. "Make free with my possessions."

"Where am I?" she demanded, trying to ignore the sudden edginess assailing her. Perhaps the better question was when would the scientists or their guard dogs arrive to take her away?

# 6

He ignored her question and poured soup into two bowls and popped bread into the toaster.

Ria watched for an instant. "Is the power on?"

"No, it goes out a lot in storms. I have a generator."

Ah, she'd wondered about the constant drone. Right now, she was hungry. Her nostrils flared as she dragged the meaty goodness past her olfactory nerve. Her stomach growled, but wariness had her hanging back. If the food contained drugs, she'd never escape him.

"Eat," he said in a firm voice. "Before the soup gets cold." The toaster popped up, and he whisked the two pieces out and placed them on a plate. He carried it to the table and set it down before pulling out a chair. He sent her an expectant look. "Sit. What is your name, anyway?"

"Ria," she said without hesitation. Not one scientist knew her by this name. They'd given her a number.

"I'm Marcus."

She hesitated an instant longer.

"You have nothing to be frightened of with me. As soon as the phone is working, I'll contact Saber. He'll be worried because I promised to call him."

She'd met Saber in the café in town. He'd offered help and sent meat now and then. He'd invited her on the runs the Feline Council organized, but she'd never gone, citing her age and tapping her walking stick to demonstrate her lack of agility. The truth—letting other shifters close invited curiosity and questions she didn't want to answer. This small town, like many others, was rife with nosiness. For almost two years, she'd lived on the outskirts of Middlemarch and kept to herself. She went into town weekly for supplies and treated herself to a coffee and scone before she headed home.

"For goodness sake, woman," Marcus said, a growl rippling through his words. "Sit and start eating."

The toast popped up, and he went to retrieve it. When he returned, she was still hovering by the chair, and he sighed but said nothing else. He pulled out the second chair, dumped the toast on the plate with the other, and sat. He picked up a spoon and dipped it into his soup.

"I am starving," he said. "I had soup earlier while you were still out, but I need to consume more calories during the cold weather to keep warm and alert."

He hadn't hesitated to eat, and she'd seen him pour the soup into the bowls. She sat and reached for the spoon with a trembling hand. The spoon clinked against the china bowl, and she spilled a little soup before she lifted it to her mouth. Rich meaty broth with a hint of vegetables danced across her taste buds. She swallowed and barely prevented her moan of pleasure.

"Have some toast. Do you want butter?"

"No, thanks," she said and diagonally cut a piece of bread. She dipped one half into the soup and took a bite. Aware of him watching, she tried to eat slowly and thought she'd managed when he returned to his meal.

"How long have you been at Mrs. Hunter's place?" he asked.

She shrugged, not wanting to give him details. He was a wolf, and his sense of smell was as good as hers. She recognized him now. He was the wolf from last week. After almost colliding with him, he'd haunted her dreams and waking hours.

He'd smelled *so* perfect that she'd experienced an absurd notion of speaking with him. Luckily, her honed instincts had kicked into gear, and she'd kept walking with scarcely a hitch in her old-person gait. At first, she'd thought the Middlemarch shifters would see through her subterfuge, but everyone saw what she wanted them to see—an elderly and reclusive feline.

She didn't care what the locals thought as long as everyone believed she was a grumpy, independent old woman who preferred her own company.

She scowled down at her soup. Unfortunately, the storm had proved her undoing, and now the wolf-man had seen her true deficient shifter form. No matter what she did, her hair color, ears, and tail remained. She shot another glance at Marcus. He had mentioned nothing, but he must've seen—her ears. The hair—she might've bluffed her way through the weird calico coloring, but the ears and tail were unusual. Peculiar. Her shift into her feline form always worked, albeit a painful process, but whenever she wanted to reverse the change, those stubborn ears and tail remained attached to her person.

48

"You have the same scent as old Mrs. Hunter," he drawled, his spoon halfway to his mouth.

Her gaze flew up to meet his, and what she saw had her heart stuttering and renewed fear swirling to life. If he guessed the truth, she'd need to start afresh elsewhere. She'd moved several times to escape capture and hated to begin again. Middlemarch suited her because other shifters resided in the town. Feline. Wolf. They didn't bother her how humans might, and they acted as a warning system. Whenever strangers behaved oddly, the shifters monitored them. Even though they didn't know it, the Middlemarch residents were her extra safety net.

"Not going to comment?"

"What do you want?"

"How about the truth? I was thinking about the possibilities while heating the soup and came up with a conclusion. You and Mrs. Hunter are the same person, and you've been pretending to be an old woman."

Ria spooned up more soup and swallowed it before dipping a piece of toast into her bowl. "I don't have to tell you anything."

"Now there's gratitude for you. I discovered you unconscious on the floor and in danger of getting swept away by a landslide. I risked my life to enter your cottage and drag you out. And not one moment too soon, either. Your house washed over the lip of the hill when the two trees pinning it in place broke under the strain of the mud and rain."

Ria stilled. "It's gone?"

"Yes, you're lucky to be alive."

Huh! Hadn't the scientists proved she was difficult to kill? They'd poked and pried and cut her enough. Her thoughts raced ahead, and she set down her spoon. "Who are you? What do you want from me?"

She pinned him with a glare, then had to glance away. The knowledge galled her, but something was appealing about this wolf. Liking someone was dangerous. The scientists used friendship as a lever to get what they wanted. Ria sucked in a breath, and, along with the meaty aroma of the soup, she got a whiff of his wild pine. Damn it. She didn't want to like him, yet the cat part of her wanted to play with him. Ria snarled silently, but her feline ignored her, letting out a loud purr that rumbled through her mind for long moments.

The man—Marcus—stared before setting down his spoon. "My name is Marcus Kerr. I am a werewolf from

Scotland, and I came to Middlemarch with my pack or what remains of them. I have a furniture building business that I share with my best friend, Rory Henderson. As for what I want from you. You're my mate. I crave your body and your soul." His brown eyes held a challenge, and the tilt of his head screamed arrogance.

Ria could only study him briefly because her cat started purring when he was in their sights. Stupid beast. Her cat was the root cause of her problems. At least until she'd discovered Middlemarch and its feline population, but she wasn't stupid enough to trust anyone. Lonely—yes—but much safer.

"No comment?" he asked drily. "I've stolen your power of speech."

"How do I know you're telling the truth?"

The wolf rolled his eyes and picked up his spoon. He shoveled in a mouthful of soup before he deigned to reply. "You can speak with my pack alpha—Rory Henderson. His mate is a feline. Question Saber Mitchell or London Drummond from the Feline Council. They'll support my story."

Either he was an excellent liar, or he was spurting honesty. He hadn't hesitated to give her names to prove his story.

"I'm not your prisoner, and you don't intend to hand me over to the scientists?"

A growl burst from him, and an expression of acute distaste etched into his features. "What the devil are you talking about? What scientists?"

"The ones who experiment on shifters," she snapped back.

For an instant, his face went slack, then his eyes bulged, and his mouth fell open. "You... You came from a science lab?"

She leaped to her feet, unable to remain still for a second longer. Her hair bristled, and her ears flattened against her head. Claws protruded from her fingertips, and she didn't care that he could see her otherness. He already knew what she was—a freak her brother had sold because he was ashamed and didn't want anyone to guess their relationship.

"Ria?"

"What?"

"On my honor, I will never harm you, and I would die before I let someone return you to a lab."

At his blunt words, which carried resentment and anger

and steadfast determination, she ceased pacing and risked a glance his way. Her feline commenced with her loud and disconcerting purrs, almost deafening her.

"Not only would I protect my mate, every local pack wolf and clan cat would safeguard you."

"I'm not your mate."

His mouth twisted, one corner of his sensual lips hitching upward. "Tell that to your feline half. She's purring up a storm."

Wait. She'd done that aloud? She shook her head hard, trying to restore clarity.

"Did you drug my soup?"

"No." He reached across the table with his spoon and calmly ate some of her soup. *Huh.* Not drugged then. This situation might take a bit more thought.

# 7

THAT SOMEONE COULD IMPRISON this woman—his mate—had a growl of fury balling in his chest. He tamped it down with difficulty and applied himself to finishing his soup.

"Do you want more?" he asked, standing. His growl burst free when she took two backward steps. "I repeat. I will never hurt you. Sit and finish your meal."

She skittered farther away from him and circled the kitchen table, so it stood between them. Against every one of his instincts, he backed off and served another portion of soup into his bowl. He took the pot and ladle to her and topped up her bowl before retreating to give her space.

She tilted her head and dragged a deep breath over her

receptors. "Why do I like your scent so much?" The words spilled from her, and she chewed her bottom lip as if she regretted the outburst. Her brow scrunched, and her nose wrinkled in the way of cats when something intrigued or perturbed them.

She looked so dang cute he fought to hide his smile. His wolf gave a happy whine. Mine. Mine. *Mine.*

"We're mates," Marcus said, watching her closely.

The furrowing of her brow deepened. "How do you know?"

How *couldn't* she know?

His curiosity increased, but he'd hate to push her so hard that she fled. He did not want her to walk away—not now that he'd discovered her.

"It's your scent. I've noticed it before when I've visited the town, but until a few days ago, when you almost knocked me over exiting the café, I hadn't put a face to the scent. Your appearance confused me, but now my attraction makes more sense."

"I'm not normal," she said.

Maybe not, but she was his mate, and he didn't mind her differences. While it was apparent she couldn't go out in public without a disguise, he was positive between him,

Rory, and Saber, they could help Ria and improve her life. Keep her safe.

"There might be ways around that. Can you shift into a cat? Do a full shift, I mean?"

"The scientists forced me to shift." She was matter-of-fact, her voice without inflection. "I didn't like it. Shifting hurt."

"My shift is uncomfortable, but the more I do it, the less painful my transformation. Most cat and wolf shifters have the same reaction when morphing to their animal form." Another thought occurred. He stepped toward the table, circling her, so he didn't scare her. He reclaimed his seat. "When did you shift last?"

She blinked. "I don't shift."

"That's not healthy," he said and spooned up the soup. He swallowed and reached for a piece of toast. He was pleased when she drifted closer and sat.

"Healthy. Not healthy." She clicked her tongue, the sharp sound showing her disapproval. "Not healthy is staying in a cage and letting the scientists control me. They put me to sleep or not as it suits them. Some cut parts off."

Marcus gaped at her. "What?"

"My tail. It came back," she said with satisfaction.

"Don't know how. With the other shifters this did not happen."

A sick sensation roiled through his belly. That sounded horrendous. Barbaric. "Where did the scientists keep you?"

"Australia."

"How did you escape?"

"One worker didn't agree with the experiments. She helped me. Gave me money."

"Did they track you?"

"No. They thought I went to America. The worker led them away, and they never caught her. She was clever."

"And have you been here in Middlemarch ever since?"

"No. I explored first and found a place I felt safe. 'Tis still dangerous, but I'm careful. I like it here and wish to stay." Ria consumed her soup and set the bowl away before giving a loud burp. She chortled, and Marcus wanted to laugh with her.

Ria was an innocent. No one had ever taught her, and she'd had to learn everything herself in the human world. She was intelligent—that was obvious. The woman had survival skills that had stood her in excellent stead when most women and men, too, would've relied on others.

"How old were you when the scientists took you?"

"Twelve." She shrugged. "I was there long before the worker helped me."

"How did you end up in the lab?"

"Ivan. My brother sold me to them."

"Your brother?"

"My father's son. He is not a nice person."

Marcus pressed his lips together, unable to say precisely what he wanted to say about her brother. "Did they give Ivan money?"

"I think so."

She didn't sound angry, but he had enough fury for both of them. For any family member to sell their kin into imprisonment... He didn't have the words to describe how despicable this man was to betray his sister. Half-sister.

"Where does your brother live?"

"I don't know. My mother and father—they died. Ivan took me to the scientists, and that is all. My life is before and after. I try not to remember the middle. It's not nice."

"Will your brother come after you? The scientists?"

"I will kill Ivan should he come. The scientists will not take me either. I refuse to let that happen."

Neither would he, but it was understandable she

wouldn't trust him. Not yet.

"You're safe with me," he reiterated.

She met his gaze this time. Her brown eyes were full of shrewd intelligence, and he understood she wasn't as innocent as his initial assumption. Her experiences had taught her not to trust, and he hated that. While she didn't accept it, she was his mate. He'd make her understand this if it was the last thing he did in this world. He'd give her love and protection and friendship. Companionship. Hope for the future.

Until this moment, he hadn't had a purpose. Not really. Yes, he wanted his and Rory's new business to do well and for their pack, who'd taken the gamble on relocating to New Zealand, to thrive, but this was more. Anticipation hummed between him and his wolf at the challenge ahead of them.

His phone rang, strident and demanding, in the silence that had fallen. He plucked it up and scanned the screen. Saber.

Ria bounded to her feet and backed away while he answered, her eyes wide. He hated the flash of terror in her—quickly hidden, but not fast enough because he spotted her fear.

"It's Saber." He swiped to answer. "Yeah, Saber."

"Marcus, is everything okay? Did you find Mrs. Hunter?"

"Yes, I found her. She's safe, but a mudslide took out her house. She's here with me." He didn't tell Saber anything else, deciding this was something better told in person. "The bridge is out, too."

"We've had problems here. The town flooded, and we have water and sewage everywhere. Storm in a Teacup is bad."

"Hell, I'm sorry."

"Not as sorry as the Feline Council. I've told them for ages that we needed improvements with our river management, vegetation maintenance, and debris clearing work. The rest of the council disagreed since we haven't had a flood for over ten years, but the planners set the town at the point where a gully merges with the valley floor. We're susceptible to flooding. Given the damage, I take no pleasure in making them eat their words."

"As soon as the floodwaters recede, I'll come down to help. I've been lucky here. A couple of downed trees, but that's all."

"Do you have enough supplies?"

"Yes, we'll be fine."

"Let me know if you have any problems."

"Thanks. At least the rain has slowed, and the thunder and lightning have moved on."

"Amen to that," Saber said.

Marcus disconnected and placed his phone on the tabletop.

"You didn't tell him anything about me," Ria said, her expression unreadable.

"No. That is something better done in person. You could return to being old Mrs. Hunter, but people will start looking sideways at us when I pay marked attention to you."

She frowned. "What sort of attention?"

Marcus stood and prowled toward her, making no effort to hide his desire or his shifter status. It was time to show her exactly what he wanted, and right now, that was a kiss.

# 8

Ria's heart drummed against her ribs, and instinct had her standing her ground, even though she wanted to run. Some long-forgotten gut feeling told her it would be a mistake to display fear or to flee.

"Good girl."

She flinched because he was way too close and way too big. He did smell fantastic, though. She loved his scent and inhaled to take another whiff.

The wolf closed the gap between them, and if she took another of those deep breaths, her breasts would rub against his broad chest. Her gaze jerked upward and somehow became entangled in his. Up close, his eyes were a warm brown with golden shards, and she swore there was something otherworldly in them.

"What are you going to do?"

"I want a kiss."

"Why? No one has wanted to rub mouths with me before."

The corners of his mouth tilted upward. He hadn't shaved for a few days, and she found herself eager to touch his jawline. Aware she was staring, she lifted her eyes again. His held a smile.

"They were blind and stupid, sweetheart. Let me show you."

Before she could protest or ask more questions, he placed one big hand on her shoulder and used the other to tip up her chin. An instant later, his mouth covered hers. His lips were soft, and they moved against her mouth, and she thought for a crazy moment that his tongue traced across her lower lip, but that couldn't be right. He repeated the move, and she gasped. Something slid past her lips.

His tongue? Yes, it was, and it rubbed and twirled against hers. Ria analyzed the sensations, and while her brain shouted about germs and that this was gross, her body behaved differently. Pleasurable feelings flickered down her torso, shocking her, surprising her, and she pressed against his body. Hmm, that felt nice. He was so hard compared to her softness. They seemed to fit like a window fastening in a latch—perfectly.

Ria held on and let the kiss continue since it wasn't terrible. Marcus made a growly sound, and it vibrated in his broad chest. He lifted his head to press his forehead against hers, and she inhaled.

His scent had changed, growing earthier and stronger. Not that it was unpleasant. She still liked his fresh pine fragrance, and now it seemed as if she enjoyed his touch. His kisses.

"Do people do that all the time?" she asked.

None of the scientists had—at least not while she was watching. Middlemarch residents hadn't kissed in front of her, but they held hands and stood close to each other. Now she understood why they might do that. Her entire body tingled from her lips to the tips of her toes. Her tail swished, confined beneath the long T-shirt he had given her to wear.

Marcus smiled. "Couples do. Mates. Sometimes friends might kiss each other on the cheek as a greeting. Like this." He demonstrated for her, and immediately, her skin tingled.

This man confused her. She searched his face and saw a hint of humor and something else that flickered too quickly for her to read or understand. Every instinct advised her to trust him, yet that wasn't her way. She relied on no one, not after leaving the scientists. The young woman scientist had helped her and explained how she should hide. She'd assisted Ria in boarding a boat that was heading for New Zealand. The woman had told her to travel farther afield, but Ria had liked this place, and once the ship reached closer to shore, she'd slipped over the side and left under her own steam. It was best if the boat owner didn't know what had happened to her.

"Where did your mind go?"

"The past," she said simply. "I don't enjoy my memories."

"Did your mother and father shift to feline? Your brother?"

"My mother, but she did not shift often."

"What happened to you?"

"I did my first shift at age eleven, which excited my parent, but when it came time for me to change back, this happened." She gestured at her ears and hair. "It wasn't easy to hide, and my brother found out. He did nothing

66

until my parents died."

"When he sold you out," Marcus snarled.

"Yes." Ria studied the anger in him, his tense muscles and taut shoulders. Without giving her actions much thought, she ducked closer and pressed a quick kiss to his cheek before darting back. She beamed at him because she'd enjoyed the activity and could see why kissing was popular. Marcus not only smelled delectable, but the friction of his skin against her mouth excited her.

"Can I kiss you again? On the mouth?" His voice was hoarse, and everything about him was solid. It made her want to knead her paws against his flesh and test that hardness.

Even as she thought this, her hands curled, and her claws protruded beneath her fingernails. She extended her fingers, willing the sharp weapons to subside into her flesh again. Her control was usually better than this.

"Can I see?" he asked, stepping nearer.

She held out her hand and found she enjoyed his closeness and the rough skin of his hands against her smoother palms. Intrigued, she seized one of his massive hands and turned it over. She ran her fingers over the calluses before glancing at him.

"I work with wood to make furniture. It makes my hands rough." He smiled, his eyes glowing even more golden than earlier.

"Why do I hunger for your scent?"

His smile broadened. "I told you. We're mates. Nature has decided we're perfect for each other."

Ria shrugged, not understanding.

"You like my scent and standing close to me, right? Or at least that is how I feel when I'm near you. I want to hold you in my arms. Kissing you is amazing, and I desire more."

"The sex stuff I read in books and see on the TV? I never understood why people did that."

Marcus made a weird sound before he said, "Yes." He cleared his throat. "Think of it this way. When you're in Middlemarch, you haven't met anyone you want to kiss or hold you? Saber, for example, or any of the other Mitchell men?"

Ria considered her words and shook her head. "When I go to Storm in a Teacup, all I am interested in is the cheese things. The scones. They are delicious, and I eat one every time I visit."

"But not the men?"

"No, I stay away." Ria frowned. "The only day I sensed

anything different was when I bumped into you on leaving the café."

"Ah, you remember me." Smugness filled his face and voice.

"Yes."

"That's good. So do you understand now about mates? What about your parents? Were they mates?"

Ria didn't know, but they had been close and died together. "I do not know. When they died, I was still young. My brother was much older."

"Have you seen him since?"

"No, I dislike him. I'd bite him and use my claws if I saw him again."

"I'd help," Marcus said, his tone holding an emotion she couldn't decipher. "We'll talk about this later. What do you want to do next?"

Ria strolled to the window and had the strange impulse to rock her hips from side to side because Marcus was watching her. Every one of her instincts told her this. Instead, she controlled herself and stared outside at the gloom. Trees had broken branches, and several had fallen, their roots now exposed, while the faint light behind her highlighted a giant puddle. Rain still pummeled the earth, and it felt like evening instead of late afternoon.

The air smelled fresher with the pine hints she caught each time she stood close to Marcus. She should go home... No, wait. Marcus had mentioned her house had suffered damage. A flash of anxiety flooded her, and a flight or fight instinct surged behind it. She whirled to Marcus, her long hair flying around her head.

"My house is gone. Where will I live?"

"You can stay with me until you decide. You're safe here."

Ria scrutinized him closely and could discern no deceit. "You do not mind me trespassing on your territory?"

"I welcome you."

Ria nodded, and another thought surfaced. "We can do more of that kissing and touching."

A slow grin spread across his mouth, and her breath caught because her heart was extra noisy and her skin prickled weirdly.

"That sounds like a fantastic plan," he said, closing the distance between them. "We should start now."

# 9

MARCUS HELD OUT HIS hand, and she didn't hesitate to put her fingers in his. He drew her closer, his wolf giving a happy little wriggle of excitement. He led her to the bedroom, all the time waiting for her to object. To his surprise, she didn't, and he found himself second-guessing his plan. This woman was an innocent and deserved goodness and sweetness in her life. She'd done well by herself but needed friends and a secure future. He was positive Saber and the Feline Council would offer help once they understood. Rory and Anita would lend their aid. Of this, he was confident.

"If the rain stops tomorrow, we might shift and run to your house. We can assess the damage."

Her eyes grew large. "You would run with me? Even though I am a freak?"

"You're not a freak," he said. "You shift in the same way I do. Would you enjoy an outing with me?"

"Yes."

"Then that's what we'll do." His wolf loved the idea of running with their mate. "As long as the weather improves. We can see if anything is salvageable."

He made a silent promise that he'd help her improve her quality of life. She shouldn't need to hide, which was what she was doing. She'd done well to date, but with his assistance and those of trusted friends, she could enjoy a more rounded life.

Marcus itched to touch her face, her lips again, so he did. He lifted her hand to his shoulder and placed it there. He tugged her close, savoring her soft curves. She wriggled against him, and he groaned. Seconds later, he kissed her, diving straight into the kiss and not hiding a jot of his arousal from her.

"What is that?" she asked when he gathered her closer. "You have something pointy down there. Is it—? Oh! I've read about these."

"It means I want you physically," he said, trying not to

laugh.

"Can I see?"

"I'll have to take off my clothes."

She gave a decisive nod and this time, a grin formed. "I don't know what a man looks like under their clothes. They only show parts on TV. Books mention more details, but I can't appreciate what they're describing."

"I see." Marcus struggled to maintain his composure. "I could do that."

"I could undress for you in return."

Marcus closed his eyes for an instant. He was counting on that, but he didn't wish to take advantage of her when she was so much younger. "Are you certain?"

"Yes, I get tingly inside and have the weird urge to flutter my eyelashes like the women on TV when I look at you. It's funny, but I've never understood that until now."

Marcus laughed, happiness flooding him. She made him smile, and he figured that apart from her lack of experience and interaction with other people, she'd gained knowledge from watching television. "You told me you can read?"

"Yes, the scientist taught me. It was one of the intelligence tests. I didn't always cooperate with their tasks, but I enjoyed books. They knew it too. I was careless, and they witnessed my joy in the printed word. They took them away as a punishment."

Bastards. "I have books. You are welcome to read as many as you like. If you don't enjoy them, we'll find some others. They have the tiny library in town. Have you looked at that?"

She wrinkled her nose. "I didn't understand what to do and didn't like to ask anyone."

Anger throbbed through him anew. She'd done everything to avoid nosy interest or recapture. "I'll answer your questions. Saber is also the perfect person to speak with, or his wife Emily would help if you had female queries. My friend Rory and his wife Anita would also offer aid. I promise—you can trust any of them. Do you understand?"

"Yes. Thank you."

Marcus dipped his head in a curt nod and unbuttoned his shirt. He tossed it aside and let Ria look her fill.

"Some men have tattoos." She looked askance at him.

"Some do. I have none."

Her gaze moved down his body and stopped when she reached the waistband of his jeans. "All your clothes. I don't mind taking off mine since I'm used to nudity. I possessed no clothes until my escape."

They'd kept her naked and studied her like an interesting bug. The bastards. "Let me take off my clothes, then you can decide." He unfastened his jeans and pulled them and his boxer briefs down his legs. Lastly, he removed his socks because wearing just socks looked plain weird. Then, he turned to face Ria and waited, his pulse unaccountably racing because her opinion mattered to him. He wanted her and had from the moment he'd caught her scent. Meeting her in person had solidified his need.

She scrutinized him closely before meeting his gaze. She licked her full lips, leaving them shiny and tempting. "Can I touch you?"

"Wherever you wish." He planted his feet and waited while her sweet, smoky scent filled each breath. Her fingers skimmed his shoulder and down his arm. She poked his biceps.

"You have more muscles than me."

"Males are stronger in all species, but females make up for it with beauty or intelligence or both."

"The scientists thought me ugly."

"You're not. Kissing you is magical, and I wish to have sex with you. I choose to take you as my mate and live with you for the rest of our lives. Do you understand?" So much honesty, but given her circumstances, he figured it was better if he set out his intentions. She, more than anyone, deserved the truth.

"What if we had children? Men and women have kids. They might be freaks like me."

"I don't consider you a freak. I've told you that. You're beautiful, but if it sets your mind at rest, our children are more likely to be wolves than felines. Offspring usually takes after the male. At least that is what I have observed."

Her chin lifted, and a flash of challenge flared in those golden eyes. "I would keep my child safe."

"We would keep our child safe," he countered. "Together and with the help of our friends."

"How? Your life wouldn't be normal with me at your side."

"I have ideas. We will have a fantastic life together. Enough talk. Now, stop worrying and touch me. I ache for the sensation of your hands sliding over my skin. Wait. Why don't you remove your clothes so we can look and touch together?"

Like the curious cat she was, she cocked her head, and her furry orange ears pricked, poking from beneath the long strands of black, white, and marmalade-colored hair. Whatever she was searching for must've reassured her because she whipped his T-shirt off and stood before him without blinking an eye.

"You're stunning," he said once he spoke. She was curvy and shapely in all the right places, her appearance human until he caught the faint flick of her black and orange tail. Ah, she wasn't as calm as she projected. He placed his hands on her shoulders and stole a kiss. Without hesitation, she pressed against him, her skin warmer than he'd expected. He skimmed his fingers down her bare back and stopped when his hand reached the base of her tail.

A soft purr rippled from her, and he smiled inwardly. Ria was amazing with her openness and honest reactions. Although she'd used subterfuge to remain hidden, he realized despite her life experiences, she preferred candor. That suited him perfectly. Without breaking their kiss, he lifted her and stalked toward his bed. Aware that she might feel cornered if he caged her with his limbs, he rearranged their bodies, so she draped on top of him.

For an instant, she stared at him with wide eyes as if seeking reassurance or trying to understand what he wanted. He couldn't decide which. Following instinct, he ran his hand down her back again, stroking her until she purred, and her tail stopped its tap-tap-tap against the covers.

"You can touch me anywhere you wish," he reminded her.

She levered away from him and studied his body. His chest. His waist. His abs. Her fingers followed her gaze, and he was glad she'd kept her claws sheathed.

"This is the part you stick inside me to make children." As she spoke, she clasped his cock.

"Not only for children but for pleasure. Both male and female should enjoy lovemaking." Marcus sucked in a deep breath and prayed he didn't explode. She wasn't doing anything except asking questions, yet every inch of him sizzled with energy and need. Rory, his friend, had explained that sex was ten times better with a mate, but Marcus hadn't understood how until now.

She dipped her head and licked across his tip, the rough drag of her feline tongue almost sending him into orbit. "You taste interesting."

"Did the scientists—?"

"No," she said, meeting his gaze. "They wished to wait until I was mature, and also, they were searching for another of my kind. They did not find one."

That was something. "Would you like me to show you how it all works?"

Ria studied his expression, and what she saw must've bolstered her because she nodded.

"There is one more thing I need to ask you. What do you know of the mating process?"

"Not much."

"Wolves and felines—at least the ones I know of—mark their mates here." He tapped on the fleshy pad where neck and shoulder met. "We do this by biting, which allows our enzymes to mix. Once this happens, the mating ties are even stronger, and only death will break the bond. Even then, from what I hear, the surviving mate finds life difficult."

"You would bite me here?"

"Yes, and you would bite me in the same way. Here." He tapped his mating site. "We won't do this today. I want to give you time to become used to me and the idea of us together. Do you understand?"

"Yes, thank you for explaining this to me. All the shifters in Middlemarch have this mark?"

"The ones who have found their mates."

"But some are human."

"Yes, in this case, the shifter will bite their mate. This gives humans greater immunity to disease and allows them to age more slowly to match their partner."

"I did not see this on TV."

"No, it is something only shifters are aware of. We keep it a secret."

She nodded. "Show me," she said, her voice imperious.

Marcus bit back a smile and rolled toward her, giving her some of his weight. He nuzzled her neck and gave her a hint of teeth at her mating site, just enough to tease.

Ria shuddered and clasped him closer. Not wanting to push, he moved on in his exploration. His fingers skimmed her shoulders and arms before drifting to her breasts. He cupped one globe and licked around the areola until he'd tormented her nipple to a hard point. Only then did he take it into his mouth and suck. Her entire body shuddered, and a purr accompanied this. Her hands settled on his shoulders, keeping him close, and his heart and wolf sang in victory. She wanted him as much as he craved her.

# 10

RIA LOVED THE WAY Marcus handled her with his abrasive hands. He stroked her with measured caresses that made her feline purr in enjoyment and her tail lazily swish. He shaped her breasts and sucked on her nipples, the wondrous sensations drifting downward until the place between her legs moistened and tingled. Marcus swapped from breast to breast while she held him close, glorying in his solid weight.

After long moments where she turned to soft mush, he moved farther down her body and parted her legs. Cool air contrasted with the heat of her flesh, and her heart thumped louder. Faster. Marcus glanced up at her and grinned as if pleased with her response. Could he hear her pulse? It was deafening. And purrs kept vibrating up her throat because his presence brought excitement and happiness.

He drew a fingertip up the inside of her thigh, and that touch leaped over her body, that one caress hitting every inch of her skin.

"Are you ready?" His voice was husky, and his eyes sparkled with humor.

Ready for what, she wanted to ask, then he dragged his finger higher across soft, damp flesh. That fingertip traced back and forth, and the sensations that raced through her were magical.

"More," she pleaded.

"You like that."

"Yes." She almost cried when he lifted his finger away, and she opened her mouth to protest.

"Shush, sweetheart," he whispered. "You'll like this, I promise."

And he slid his hands under her butt and lifted her. He licked the flesh he'd touched mere seconds ago. The lap of his tongue was light, and it danced across her skin, firing sensitive nerve endings to life. He concentrated on a tender spot, and decadent pleasure shot through her. A purr emerged from deep in her throat—one sound that meant she was thrilled. Marcus continued to lick her, but he also slid a finger inside her, and these sensations combined until everything contracted into a tight ball. An instant later, that mass exploded, and her body pulsed in time with her rumbling breaths.

Marcus pulled back to study her. She felt the weight of his stare and realized she'd closed her eyes. She opened them and met his sparkling gaze and bright smile.

"How was that?" He released her hips and let her drop to the mattress. Another purr escaped her.

"I liked it, but I thought there was more."

"There is," Marcus said. "Are you ready for me to show you now?"

"Yes." And she was excited about it. While she'd seen other men in the town, not one of them had tempted her to try the situations she'd witnessed on TV. Until Marcus.

"Right then. Lie on your back. Yes, like that. Now, part your legs for me. Ria?"

"Yes." Her gaze shot to his face.

"If you want me to stop, all you need to do is tell me. Or if I do anything you don't like, let me know, and I'll stop."

He was more powerful than her but didn't frighten her.

Everything about Marcus appealed to her—his wolfish scent, his appearance, his smile, and his honest eyes. She could tell a lot about a person from their eyes and seldom was she wrong.

"Ria? Did you hear what I said?"

"Marcus, I want this. I need you." Nothing but the truth.

"Thank the stars," he said.

He stroked and kissed her everywhere, but when she tried to return the exploration, he guided her hands back to the mattress.

"Why can't I touch you?" she demanded, stymied for the third time by his determination and superior strength. Not that he was hurting her. He merely gripped her wrists and refused to let her move.

"Because if you touch me, there's a danger I'll lose control and simply take you. I want you to crave me and your body to be soft and ripe with wanting. Hurting you is not an option."

She stared at him, weighing his words, and discovered truth and honesty. "The men on TV don't linger and move slower than the snails in my garden."

He huffed out a laugh and attracted her attention to his

chest. Of course, her gaze wandered downward and stilled at his erection.

"Your male part is in a hurry."

He snorted, this sound carrying humor, and kissed her mouth, sipping at her lips and distracting her with his fingers at her breasts. He squeezed her nipple to a point shy of pain, and that minor irritation darted down her body, making her hips lift restlessly and her flesh throb with a needy hunger.

She settled her hands on his shoulders, pleased that he'd released them. His skin was warm to her touch, and his wild pine scent surrounded her.

He parted their lips and reached over to get something. Ria's eyes widened as she watched him roll a condom down his shaft.

"It's time," she said with a grin.

"It is." His eyes glowed golden, and she thought she spotted the flicker of his wolf peeking out at her. A hum rumbled up her throat, a sound of happiness and acceptance.

"Now remember this. The first time can be painful, and I'll do my best not to hurt you too much." He fitted his cock to her and pushed.

Ria held her breath, waiting for the pain, but it didn't come—at least not in the amount she'd expected.

"Okay?"

She nodded and gripped his shoulders. She wanted his mouth against hers again and decided there was no reason to wait for him. Ria pressed her lips to his and kissed him in the way he'd shown her. To her immense satisfaction, he groaned, and his hips surged forward, forcing his cock deeper. Her hands tightened on his shoulders, and he stilled.

"Keep going," she said against his mouth. "I like this. It feels amazing."

He withdrew a fraction before sliding fully inside her. A sense of fullness assailed her, but it wasn't unpleasant—not when he twisted to the right. He rubbed against a spot that had her gasping and quivery with acute anticipation.

"More," she ordered.

Marcus laughed, but he took direction well. He pulled back and thrust until he could go no further. He cupped her face and stared into her eyes. Yes, that was his wolf. Intelligence and strength—she saw that too. This closeness and intimacy with Marcus—she liked it, and now some things she'd seen on her TV made more sense.

Marcus pulled out of her, and she gripped his shoulders in a silent but urgent protest.

"Steady, sweetheart. I won't stop." And as if to prove he meant it, he thrust into her again, hitting the same spot that made her see stars. He retreated and invaded her body, and she strove to meet his strokes. The faint pain from the start had dispersed, and instead, each of his thrusts lit her nerve endings. *So good*. Now she understood why people did this sex thing. It was wondrous.

"More," she demanded.

Marcus's husky laugh thrilled her, as did his obeying her instructions. The sensations tugged into a tight knot in her abdomen.

She was vaguely aware of renewed rain on the roof, but the knowledge drifted away, and everything about Marcus consumed her. That ball of pleasure grew and continued to contract, pulling at her senses and making her feel as if she danced on a knife's edge. Marcus kissed her, his tongue tangling with hers while he continued thrusting into her. The pressure coalesced to the point of no return, and the tangle of sensations in her exploded, shattering and streaking down her legs and body.

Her breaths came in harsh pants against his lips, and she tore her mouth from his to breathe. Weirdly, that tangle of sensations had built again, and she groaned, unsure if her body could take more. Instead, she licked down his throat, and the strangely pleasurable spasms that continued in her lower body seemed to make Marcus move faster. She gripped his shoulders and savored the salt on his skin. She nibbled his neck, and he pushed into her with greater strength.

The pleasure intensified, and she bit down as she attempted to contain the scream that tried to exit as she climaxed again. Marcus groaned and stilled above her, his entire body shaking. Ria tasted blood in her mouth and instinctively lapped across the wound she'd created. She wasn't sure why she'd bitten him, but he didn't seem to mind. His bigger body shuddered against hers every time her tongue stroked the mark.

Gradually, Marcus's trembling ceased, and he drew away, parting their bodies. He stood and removed the condom, then walked from the room. She stared after him, wondering what happened next. On TV, the couples cuddled, and she thought that might be nice because she felt sleepy.

Somewhere close, water ran from a pipe, slightly louder than the rain that struck the roof. Ria closed her eyes, more relaxed than she'd ever been. This sex business was a lot of fun, and she looked forward to doing it again with Marcus.

# 11

SHE'D CLAIMED HIM.

Marcus's heart sang with happiness, although confusion filled him too. He'd thought she understood the mating concept, but when she'd bitten him, she'd surprised him. Every part of him had screamed to return the favor because he had no doubts. She was an innocent in so many ways and years younger. He'd chosen to give her time.

He removed the condom, relieved nothing hinky had happened. Rory and Ramsay had both told him they'd knotted inside their mates, but that was a complication he could do without. A relationship with Ria came with enough problems, not that this worried him.

He had nil doubts.

Marcus grabbed a flannel and dampened it with warm water. He strode back into his bedroom and found Ria curled on her side and fast asleep. Her striking-colored hair spilled across his pillow, and she seemed impossibly youthful. Beautiful. His fingertips stroked his new mark, and a shiver ran through him, a spike of sensation following close behind. Hell. This woman.

Given he was now in his thirties, he'd wondered if he'd ever find his mate. Ria was much younger in experience and age, but she was his to keep safe. He crawled into bed and tugged the covers over them, but Ria didn't waken. Marcus wasn't tired, his mind too busy working out how Ria could have a more normal life yet remain safe. His first thought, once again, was to speak with Saber and lay out the facts. There must be some way to protect this incredible woman from harm and exploitation. Given that she'd hidden for years, she'd had few opportunities for formal education.

If she wanted, the community could and would help her.

THE NEXT DAY, THE rain eased off, and although the

clouds remained dark and forbidding, Marcus asked Ria if she'd like to run with him to her place. They could see about retrieving her possessions, and while they were down that way, check the stream. While a vehicle crossing was impossible, they might ford the water on foot if the level wasn't too high.

"Yes," Ria said with enthusiasm. "I'd love to shift to my cat form."

"Let's go now before it rains again." Marcus whipped his T-shirt over his head and bent to tug off his socks before he knew Ria was staring. "What?"

"Looking at you makes me happy."

He grinned. "Hurry so that I can look at you."

"Not much to see. The scientists told me this."

"They were idiots and lacked imagination. I enjoy watching you. No one else's opinion matters. Now hustle, woman, or I'll go without you."

Marcus finished disrobing and walked outside. Ria joined him a short time later, and after shutting the door, he curled her against his side and nuzzled her neck. She laughed and let him for an instant before she backed away and shifted.

Marcus shifted too and silently noted her process

was slower than his and uncomfortable. Once her transformation completed, she was smaller than the adult black leopard shifters who lived in Middlemarch. Her coloring made her stand out. She bore black, orange, and white patches in similar shades to her hair. Given the colors of the landscape, she'd blend well, which was something.

He set off at a trot and took the straightforward route along the gravel road. With the bridge out, traffic was unlikely, and they'd hear a vehicle in time to hide should someone drive this way. It took twenty minutes to reach Ria's road.

Ria let out a low grunt, and Marcus slowed. She took the lead, and he followed, his wolf supremely happy at spending time with his mate. Ria led him to a gate and jumped over, before turning to see if he had followed her. He had, and he nuzzled her flank, silently urging her to continue. They sloshed through puddles, trotted along a grassy, tree-lined ridge, and finally stopped at a rocky outcrop.

Marcus halted beside Ria as she gazed into a water-filled valley. The remnants of her cottage lay strewn on rocks, the rest presumably swept away with the surge of flood water.

Marcus shifted, but Ria didn't follow suit. "Do you

want to investigate the stream? We have enough food for two or three more days, but it might be best if we try to go to town. Saber says the town flooded, and they'll need help."

She sat on her haunches and stared at him, giving him a feline curl of lips.

Marcus thought quickly. She couldn't continue living the way she had been. Surely, she understood that. Hers had been a lonely life, always, with the possibility of danger from the scientists scurrying through her mind.

He straightened his shoulders and took a risk. "You can remain here if you're too frightened to go into town, but Rory and Anita won't mind if we stay with them for a few days. They'll help us with clothes and a disguise for you. You'll be among my pack and my friends. I would trust any of them with my life."

Ria shifted, and he waited patiently until she stood in her human form. "I do not wish to go to town."

"You bit me." He caressed the scar. "You claimed me, and you can't undo this."

"You didn't claim me," she shot back, and he would've sworn hurt lingered in her voice, although she hadn't mentioned this earlier.

"I intend to, but I wanted to give you time. This is new to you, and I get you must take care. But I can't live in isolation. Wolves are pack animals and do better with family and friends around."

"I wouldn't stop you from seeing your friends."

He cupped her face, not sure how to make her understand. "A mating bond is the closest and tightest tie there is. When I mark you, I want you to join my pack and get to know my friends—the people I trust. This is a safe place, and not one of them would betray you."

"Say you," she said. "My brother sold me for hard cash. The scientists informed me of this."

"We have more to lose than your brother because we're shifters too. We'll work out a better disguise for you, and you can come and go from town. I can even take you farther afield. Perhaps to Dunedin, which is our nearest city. Wouldn't you like to explore more of the world?"

"Yes," she said simply. "But if the scientists recapture me, you might suffer."

"I would, but I'm trying to say that you no longer need to be alone. I stand at your side."

Her expression suggested she didn't believe him, but it was early days. Besides, no matter what she thought, she'd claimed him, and he wasn't going anywhere.

"Let's shift again and check out the stream. I bet I can beat you."

Her eyes gleamed, and she started her shift. Marcus paused, congratulating himself because his mate was competitive. He grinned after her, admiring the flick of her tail and her agility as she raced away.

Marcus shifted and bolted along the ridge and down the hill after Ria. He slowly carved away at the distance between them and caught her as they approached the crossing.

Of the former bridge, there was no sign. Muddy water spilled over the bank in places, the surge of the stream full of broken branches and other debris. Ria's sides heaved as she stood beside him, and unable to help himself, he leaned into her, savoring her scent and closeness. While the breadth was wider than usual here, farther along, the swift current had cut more deeply into the earth, and he thought they could leap over without difficulty.

Movement on the other side of the stream snared his attention. A wolf and a feline. Rory and Anita. And Toby, their adopted son, was with them too, hopping along on three legs. They trotted toward the water, and Ria tensed, halting. He wanted to tell her it was all right, but since he couldn't speak to her right now, he leaned into her and guided her onward. She dug in her feet and fought him, but he used his greater strength.

Finally, he stopped and shifted and spoke to her. "This is my closest friend, Rory, his mate, Anita, and their son, Toby. We need to speak with them. Please." He waited until the tension left her body before he walked to the bank.

"Rory!"

Rory shifted. "I was wondering how you were getting on. Who is with you? I thought Saber asked you to check on Mrs. Hunter."

"I did and found something unexpected. This is Ria, my mate." Rory's mouth dropped open, and Marcus laughed. "We only have one, maybe two days of food left. How are your supplies?"

"Your mate?" His brow knit with confusion.

"Ria and I will jump the stream farther down." He gestured to the left. "Can we stay with you? How is the town? Saber got a quick call through and mentioned the flood. I figured he could do with cleanup help."

"You can stay with us. Anita did a big shop the day

before the storm. We've been lucky and have escaped any damage. You?"

"Ria lost her house in a mudslide. I had a tree fall, but other than that, things are good at my place." Marcus set his hand on Ria's shoulder and squeezed lightly to snare her attention. "Are you okay? We'll be safe with Rory and Anita. I promise you."

Ria growled, but before they could speak further, another wolf and a cat appeared behind Rory.

Ria vibrated with tension and retreated, but Rory stayed her with his hand. "These are more friends. Shift, sweetheart. Tell me what you want to do. I get this is scary for you, but they've seen you now."

# 12

PANIC ROARED THROUGH RIA. Her tail flicked from side to side, and her claws extended deep into the mud beneath her paws. She backed up two steps, and Marcus moved with her.

"Ria, please. They're my friends. I trust them with my life and promise you'll be protected."

Her brother had told her he was taking her to safety. She'd believed him, but then she'd still been a child and unwise to the world's ways. The scientists had stripped her trust and taught her that even the most innocent of occurrences could come back to bite with razor-sharp teeth.

"How about this?" Marcus squatted in front of her and

pressed his forehead to hers. "If you feel unsafe, I'll help you leave again. I can give you money and anything else you require."

She glanced past him and noticed the child for the first time. Her gaze narrowed, focusing on the much smaller wolf. He had only three legs. She studied him for long seconds, observing how each adult took care not to jostle him. They nuzzled him with affection, and even more astounding, he greeted the two newcomers, and they treated him with the same kindness.

Marcus was right when he told her that these shifters faced the same danger as her. The trust had to go both ways. She'd reserve judgment—for now.

Ria halted her retreat and licked Marcus's hand to show compliance.

"Thank you," he said in a low voice. "We'll jump the stream at the narrowest point over there."

Ria trotted toward the area Marcus had indicated and increased her speed. She heard Marcus curse and flicked her tail. A heartbeat later, Ria sprang and hurtled over the racing water. She landed lightly and kept moving, so she didn't provide an obstacle for Marcus.

Marcus followed and raced up to her, snapping his teeth

and demonstrating his displeasure. Ria smirked, every instinct telling her he was all show. Immediately on the tail of this thought came the knowledge she'd already trusted him. In the time they'd been together, he'd treated her with care and had taken great pains not to frighten her. He'd saved her. Yes, these shifters were as vulnerable as she was with people like the scientists.

Marcus greeted his friends, including the pup. She sensed their curiosity, but they trotted away from the stream, and Marcus nudged her to follow. She loped after the group, curious about the dynamics between the wolves and the leopards. The adults kept the pup safe in the middle of their group, and they traveled at his pace.

Watching this warmed Ria's heart. If they cared this much for a different and weaker pup, they might embrace her differences or at least ignore them.

Her thoughts whirled like eddies in the raging stream, and they seesawed between cautious trust and paralyzing fear that sent chills writhing through her veins. What if one of Marcus's friends—? No. *No.* That made little sense. They bore similar secrets to her, and she'd never noticed or heard anything troubling when she lived in Middlemarch. And she listened closely when she made her brief trips to town to purchase supplies and sell the knitted items she made to support herself. At first, eavesdropping had been why she'd visited the café, but soon she went as a treat since the owner's cheese scones were tasty. While the shifters had acknowledged her, they'd given her space and hadn't poked into her privacy. Yet Saber—the leader—had also made it clear if she required help to ask.

The wolf at the front of their group traveled through the sodden landscape, past large schist formations, and through tussock grass. At specific points, he surveyed the landscape, and she approved of his caution. The wind whistled over the brow of the hill, and the somber clouds sinking low on the horizon hinted at yet more rain to come. They paused once more when a vehicle drove slowly down a rutted gravel road, each sinking to their bellies and freezing in position in the tussock. Ria followed suit, her heart pounding. She seldom shifted because it reminded her of the scientists. Dreadful memories, yet setting out with Marcus today hadn't bothered her as much as usual.

Once Ria could no longer hear the vehicle, the wolf in the lead rose and headed deeper into the valley. They rounded a knoll, and she caught sight of a house nestled at the base of a neighboring hill. The storm damage didn't seem as bad in this valley, although mud splattered with every step and covered her fur.

The leading wolf veered in the house's direction, and Ria followed with the rest of their group. Once they were at the rear of the house, everyone shifted, apart from Ria. She was staring at the child, who was missing part of his arm. She glimpsed him before he scooted indoors. The woman followed him, and she heard the rush of water inside. A shower?

Ria hesitated, not wanting to shift because the idea of everyone staring at her brought a wash of nerves. She was abnormal. Different. None of these shifters kept their tails when they morphed into their human forms. The scientists were right. She was an oddity. A freak.

Marcus spoke with the men before one disappeared inside. The other two grabbed clothes from a parked vehicle and hurriedly dressed before leaving.

Ria stared after the truck, and Marcus must've understood her concern.

"They're off to help with the town cleanup. Saber said the café flooded."

Storm in a Teacup? That was bad because she eagerly anticipated her cheese scones.

"Come inside out of the cold. Rory and Anita are getting clothes for us."

Rory appeared with an armful of garments. He'd already taken a quick shower, judging by his damp hair.

"Anita is with Toby in our en suite. I brought you a robe," Rory said. "You can go to the bedroom, and Anita will have clothes for you. Marcus, you use the shower in the main bathroom. I'll put on the kettle and set the table for lunch."

"Shift, sweetheart. I've known Rory since we were the same age as Toby."

What ifs still plagued her, yet this was precisely how she felt each time she ventured into town, and she'd been doing that for ages. Her appearance didn't bother Marcus, but what about the others? This was so hard.

"Remember, if it gets too much for you, I'll take you home to my place. At the very least, we'll have a hot lunch before we go out in the storm."

Ria started. She hadn't even noticed the pelt of the rain against the windows. She huffed in a breath and smelled food and what seemed suspiciously like cheese scones. This hesitation was stupid. She had to keep telling herself that the other shifters had known she was like them each time she'd gone into town. Yes, they'd thought her old, but they'd treated her decently. And she was lonely.

There—she'd admitted this truth to herself.

It had hovered when she'd seen the women talking together and laughing, enjoying themselves. The men and women interacted. Even the children had played and laughed and cried and laughed some more. They'd all been shifters.

It was time to take a chance and extend a little trust.

Ria shifted.

"Good girl." Marcus kissed her. It was a quick kiss and left her craving more. Her disappointment must've shown because he gave her a peck and picked up an item of clothing. "Put this on." He held up the robe and helped her don it.

Ria's legs trembled, but she forged onward with slow footsteps along a carpeted passage. She entered the bedroom and came to a halt. The boy's chortle rang out. He was different, and they still cared for him. Her mouth had turned dry, but she didn't flee as every instinct urged.

Marcus was right, and returning to a solitary life made her want to cry. Which meant she needed to travel in another direction.

"Hello." Even to Ria, her voice sounded hesitant, but the woman heard and lifted her head. Her smile froze on her face, and Ria's stomach churned with fear and nerves. *Run!* Except her feet didn't obey her brain. She was tired of running. She dragged in a huge breath and let it ease out slowly. "Hello, my name is Ria. Do you have clothes that will hide my tail and ears? I want to make Marcus proud."

"Oh, honey," the woman said. She turned to the boy and finished turning up the empty sleeve, so it didn't flap around. "Off you go. Help Rory and Marcus with lunch."

"Thank you, Anita." He clattered from the bedroom.

Anita rose from the corner of the bed. "How about a pair of baggy track pants? Your ears are fine for now. It's just Rory, Toby, and me, and none of us would ever gossip, but let me see." She rifled through a drawer. "Ah-ha!" She picked up a black item and turned with a flourish. "This hat should work. It looks stupid on me, but I think it will work for you and hide your ears. When I saw you in your feline form, I was curious about your hair color. It's gorgeous. Very striking."

"People stare," Ria said.

"Jealousy is a bad thing."

"I don't think they were jealous. They thought I was a

freak."

"Well, they were wrong. Once we sort out the flood damage, we'll visit Caroline at her shop and see what she can do to help you. She is a brilliant designer."

"Caroline. I know her." She lifted her gaze to Anita and saw nothing but friendly interest. The distaste and disgust she used to surprise on the scientists' faces wasn't on Anita's. Hope surged in her. "Do you think Caroline would help? She buys my knitting and sells it in her shop. Except I'll need to purchase more needles and yarn since I've lost everything."

"You do her knitting? She told me an elderly shifter lady does it for her." Anita stared at Ria, and her eyes widened.

Ria quaked inside and blinked.

"You're elderly Mrs. Hunter?" Her attention focused on Ria's ears and hair. "Oh, that explains a lot. Don't worry. Caroline is always raving about your products and says she can't keep the shelves stocked because every time a tourist bus comes through, the customers buy everything she has."

Ria hadn't believed Caroline when she'd mentioned the same thing. Caroline had also told her she wasn't charging enough. When Ria had tentatively increased her prices,

Caroline had given her even more and told Ria she was still making a handsome profit. Ria respected Caroline. Before coming to Middlemarch, she had received far less money for her work.

Anita handed her a pile of clothes and a hat. "I can help you put your hair up so it tucks underneath, and the hat band will hide the unique position of your ears."

Anita was matter-of-fact, and she didn't poke fun or jeer. She didn't stare, and by the time Ria had dressed, she wasn't feeling as self-conscious.

"Lunch is ready!" Toby clattered along the passage and hollered from the doorway.

"We're coming right now," Anita said.

Ria followed Anita into a large kitchen. Marcus sat with Rory and Toby at a wooden table big enough to seat eight.

"Ria, take a seat beside Marcus," Anita said and slipped into the chair next to Rory.

"Okay?" Marcus murmured.

Ria's stomach did a slow flip, and she offered him a smile and a nod. He reached beneath the table and squeezed her knee.

She ate her tomato soup and spread butter on her scones, the entire experience surreal. This must be how it felt to be normal, and it was within her grasp. All she needed to do was trust in Marcus and his friends.

# 13

"WE'RE GOING INTO TOWN to help with the cleanup," Marcus said. "Rory heard they'd arranged for the road clearance now that the rain has slowed. Do you want to come?"

Ria hesitated, still worried about opening herself up to others in the community. The lady scientist who'd helped her to escape had told her to trust no one, that she would always be in danger, but the last few days had reinforced the fact she was lonely and craved more from life than what she discovered from TV programs. Plus, Marcus gave her confidence, and the barest notion of him leaving her had her stomach tap-dancing with nausea.

"You can stay here," Anita said.

"No!" The word burst from Ria. "I wish to go with you. I will help."

Marcus's smile of approval warmed her all over, and he squeezed her leg again, leaving his hand resting on her thigh. Ria bit into her cheese scone, and she was at ease for the first time in as long as she could recall.

The drive into Middlemarch was slow, given the state of the road leading to the country town. Before entering the main street, they splashed through puddles and bumped over stones and other foreign debris.

"Wow, Saber said the flood was bad," Anita said from the front of the vehicle. "It looks as if the water has poured through the shops. Oh, there's Caroline and Marsh. Can you let Ria and me off here? We'll help them."

Rory obediently halted on the shoulder.

"Toby, do you want to go with us or remain with Rory and Marcus?"

"Stay with Rory," Toby said.

"We'll call you when we're ready to leave," Rory said.

Marcus leaned closer and kissed the tip of Ria's nose. "Will you be all right?"

She hesitated.

"You can get Anita to call me, and I'll come immediately.

Okay?"

Ria nodded, and Marcus stole another kiss before releasing her. "See you later."

Ria kept step with Anita as she headed for Caroline's shop.

"Caroline. We've come to help," Anita said. "This is Ria Hunter."

"Oh, good. Marsh promised he'd help Saber, so I'd be glad of the extra hands." She smiled at Ria. "You picked a bad time to visit. Are you staying with Anita and Rory?"

"Yes," Ria said, hesitating.

"Can we talk inside?" Anita asked.

Caroline glanced from Ria to Anita and back. "Ah, sure," she said and led the way inside.

The floor was wet but clean, with stock piled on counters and shelves.

"Did you lose any stock?" Anita asked.

"Marsh told me he thought this would be bad and to prepare, so I packed most of my dresses and took them home. A fantastic decision. A little water came under the door and brought silt, but the stock damage is minimal." She paused, staring at Ria. "Have we met before? Something about you is familiar."

"I..." Ria stopped, took a deep breath, and started again. Caroline had been fair in their dealings together and struck Ria as an honest person. "I am Mrs. Hunter. I knit for you."

Caroline's mouth opened before she snapped it shut again. She shook her head. "Why did you pretend to be elderly? Your disguise... I never once suspected."

Ria glanced at Anita, and her new friend sent her an encouraging smile. Ria reached up to tug off her hat and steeled herself for an adverse reaction.

"Wow, your hair is an amazing color, but I don't see—ah! Your ears."

"I have a tail, too," Ria said.

"You've been hiding in plain sight," Caroline said. "I understand."

"Marcus has talked Ria into being more sociable with those in the shifter community. They're mates," Anita said with a smile.

"You'll need outfits to disguise your differences," Caroline said. "I'd be happy to help as long as you keep knitting your beautiful garments for me."

"Deal," Ria said and replaced her hat to hide her ears.

By the time Marcus and Rory arrived to take them

home, they'd set Caroline's store back in order. All Caroline required was to restock her shelves and open for business.

Ria and Anita waved goodbye and piled into the vehicle.

"How is Storm in a Teacup?" Anita asked.

"It's still a mess, but most water is out, and the floor is drying. It will be at least another week before the café can reopen. They'll do a deep clean first and replace some furniture and equipment," Rory reported.

Marcus grasped Ria's hand and curled his fingers around hers. "How did you go?"

She beamed at him. "You were right. I need to give the local shifters a chance to get to know me. Caroline offered to design clothes to help me blend in with other people."

"You can gradually meet the other shifters, and when we go on our next run, come too," Marcus said.

"I'd like this." Nothing less than the truth. Although she didn't want to kid herself and think integrating would be easy, she already had friends who'd help, which gave her a warm sensation in her chest.

"I spoke with Saber. I didn't think you'd mind since he is a community leader. He told me he thought there was something odd with you but couldn't put his finger on what it was."

"Huh!" Ria said.

"He suggested we meet with him later in the week. He said Emily would want to meet you, so they'd invite us for dinner. Is that all right with you?"

"Yes." Ria never hesitated. On this one afternoon, her confidence had grown, and she finally accepted her life could be better and more enjoyable. "Thank you, Marcus."

"You don't need to thank me, sweetheart. Finding you has made me happy and given me a purpose."

Ria leaned in and kissed him. She thought she loved this man, and once they were alone, she'd tell him so. With Marcus at her side, the future looked bright, and she couldn't wait to experience new things with her mate.

# 14

AFTER AN ENJOYABLE DINNER, drinks and chatter, while sitting in front of the fire, Marcus and Ria retired to the room Anita had told them to use.

"Have you had an enjoyable day, sweetheart?"

"Immensely," she said, unable to stop smiling.

Marcus drew her against his chest. "You are an amazing woman, and even though we've known each other for mere days, I'm halfway in love with you. It won't take me much to topple the rest of the way."

Ria understood the sentiment since every time she glanced at this wolf, her heart raced, and tingles flared to life in her. Lust and wanting. Her fingers slipped beneath his shirt collar and traced over the raised bump her bite had left on his skin. He shuddered, and a groan escaped him.

"Right," he said, and his brown eyes twinkled. He stepped back and unfastened his shirt without taking his gaze off her. His socks, trousers, and underwear disappeared next until he stood in front of her naked. "Your turn. I want to make love to my beautiful mate." He hesitated. "I don't have any condoms with me, but we can still enjoy each other."

"You would want to have a child with me?"

"Yes."

She frowned. "What if they can't shift properly?"

"Remember, the offspring of shifter couples normally take after the father, which would mean, in our case, we'd have wolf pups rather than kittens."

"They would be like you."

"Most likely, but even if they take after you, I would love them. I don't think you understand how special you are. You have an inner core of strength and goodness that the scientists should have extinguished but, by a miracle, didn't. You're intelligent and industrious, and you're beautiful. Any child you have will have many fine qualities, and I would be proud to be their father."

Ria's senses worked in overdrive, and she experienced a

lightness in her chest. She was excited about a future with Marcus. She gave in to the urge that told her to touch him. "It would honor me to have your child. Our child. We do not have to use a condom."

"Are you sure you don't want more time to get used to your new life?"

"No. I want you to bite me here." She tapped her mating site. "We should claim each other."

His smile was slow and lit his entire face, mesmerizing her with his stark male beauty. "I didn't think I had a mate until I found you."

Marcus lifted the hem of her blue T-shirt and whisked it over her head. He stripped off the rest of her clothes and left them puddled on the floor. He scooped her off her feet and placed her in the middle of the mattress before following her down. Their bodies slid together, and Ria savored the weight of him and his firm muscles. He kissed her mouth and her nose, her neck with tiny kisses that were tantalizingly brief. A low moan built in her throat and spilled free when he gave her the scrape of teeth across her mating site. She shuddered helplessly, clinging to his shoulders and moving her hips against him in silent demand. His touch sent a primitive throb through her veins, as did the swollen hardness of his arousal. She put a tentative hand on his thigh, but he stopped kissing her and lifted his head.

"Hands on my shoulders," he ordered. "This is not the time to poke the bear."

"But you're a wolf."

"Let me rephrase. Don't push me. I'm hanging onto my control by a hairsbreadth. I want you to remember the day I marked you and bound us together with excitement and fond smiles. Now, keep your hands there."

"Yes, Marcus."

He stilled and made a dark sound that thrilled her. Not a shred of fear sparked to life. That was trust, and the flare of desire she saw shining in his eyes gave her confidence too.

Marcus kissed her more, tangling their tongues together and driving her crazy. His piney, masculine scent filled each of her breaths, and she loved the saltiness of his skin. Frissons of excitement gripped her as she writhed beneath his greater weight. Her tail thumped a rhythm against his thigh when he ran his fingers through her hair and stroked her ears. He raked his tongue across the swell of her stomach and moved lower to taste her. The slide of his lips against her flesh shot an arrow of heat through her, a surge of urgency. She tried to lift into his next stroke, but he cupped one hip and held her in position.

"Marcus." His name was a soft protest.

In answer, he moved back up her body and settled between her thighs. He fit his cock to her entrance and slowly pushed inside her. This time, there was no pain, no discomfort, and Marcus slid deep with ease. Once he was situated, he paused, and she relished the sense of fullness and the way his heart thudded against hers. His deep, faintly unsteady breaths told of his uncertain control, but she let him lead. Next time, she'd ask for her turn.

Finally, he started moving, withdrawing, and filling her body repeatedly until the sensations built one on top of the other, the pleasure growing with each stroke. The tightening and the wetness between her thighs increased until she thought she could no longer bear it, then suddenly, the decadent rush of feelings and emotions burst, shattering her into a maelstrom of pleasure.

It seemed to be the signal Marcus was waiting for because the pace of his thrusts increased. He lowered his head and kissed her tenderly before sliding his lips down her throat. The fingers of one hand lifted, and he placed her digits on the mark she'd bestowed on him.

Instinctively, she knew to caress it, and his muscular body tensed beneath hers. His teeth scraped across the pad of flesh at the base of her neck, and without warning, he bit down. Pain dug its claws deep, but before she had time to protest, the agony subsided, leaving only pleasure. Another series of spasms had her tightening around his cock, but there was something more. An intuitive understanding of Marcus, and how much he needed her, how much he cared for her and wanted a future for them.

It was a meeting of their minds.

The passion between them quieted, and Marcus separated their bodies. He tugged her back against him and pulled the covers over them.

"Mine," he said with quiet satisfaction.

"Yes," she agreed and closed her eyes, secure in his arms and his love. He was her mate, and she couldn't wait to enjoy the future at his side. Together.

THANK YOU FOR READING MY ELUSIVE MATE, which is part of my Middlemarch Gathering series.

Marcus, the hero of this romance, also appears in MY HIGHLAND MATE, the first book in the series. (https://shelleymunro.com/books/my-highland-mate)

Along with feline and wolf shifters, I also write dragon romances with a distinct New Zealand flavor. They're based on the legendary taniwha, the subject of many myths and legends I read while growing up. Please turn the page for a first chapter sneak peek of BLUE MOON DRAGON, book one in the Dragon Investigators series.

# Excerpt—Blue Moon Dragon

"Good morning, George Taniwha Investigators and Security." Emma forced a bright smile and hoped her despondency didn't crawl down the telephone line. Twenty-five years old today.

*Twenty-five!*

And she still hadn't plucked up the courage to approach Jack Sullivan and ask him out on a date—despite this being the age of equal opportunity. The male in question sauntered past her desk and strode into George Taniwha's office without giving her a second glance.

A man to die for...

Emma sighed and stared at the bronze nameplate on

the door in frustration. So, she wasn't the most beautiful woman in New Zealand. She was built with the word generous in mind. A large ass and a chest made to house her big heart. Or at least that was what her high school boyfriend had informed her. He'd also told her she had a nice smile and that he enjoyed being with her because she never stressed about her size. Yep, she was a normal, healthy woman—kind to animals and small children. Most people liked her, yet the wretched man ignored her existence.

"Are you there, young lady?"

The querulous voice jerked Emma from her grievances re the lack of sex life back to her phone call. "I'm sorry. I had to sign for a courier parcel," she fibbed. "How can I help you?"

"My name is Elisa Denning. I need the services of a private investigator. Someone is stealing my prize rose blooms. Right before the flower show too. It's disgraceful. That's what it is."

"Let me take some details, then I'll arrange for an investigator to come and see you. Address? Telephone number?" Emma jotted down the woman's particulars, an imp inside her laughing as she imagined George assigning this case. None of the men would appreciate chasing a rose thief. George Taniwha's operatives preferred the dangerous stuff that challenged them and proved they were men.

Her humor died, replaced by a frown that drew her brows together. That was another thing she wanted to change. She'd passed all her private investigator exams. George had promised she'd be able to take on cases soon. Perhaps this one. Never let anyone say Emma Montrose didn't have ambition.

"When can I expect someone?" the elderly lady questioned. "I'm sure it's Mrs. Gibb's grandson, but the police won't do anything."

"An investigator will contact you tomorrow morning, Mrs. Denning."

"Excellent. Tomorrow is my baking day. I'll make them a cup of tea once they arrive."

Emma couldn't restrain a grin as a vision of one of George's tough he-man investigators drinking tea from a bone china cup popped into her mind. "I'm sure they'll enjoy refreshments. Thanks, Mrs. Denning." She disconnected and transcribed two proposals for prospective clients while she waited for Jack to leave George's office. She was smitten enough to want to gaze her fill as he departed since he had a truly fine butt.

The hands of the clock moved at the pace of a sick snail, and still Jack remained in George's inner sanctum. Reluctantly, Emma packed up for the day. She grabbed her bag and couldn't prevent a glance at the closed door, searching for the tall, dark-haired man of her dreams.

Oh, yeah. No doubt about it. She was a sad, sad woman.

"I HAVE A CASE for you," George said.

Something in his boss's tone, the watchful air in his sharp brown gaze made Jack cautious. "Yeah?"

"Sports-enhancing drugs. Rumor says there's a ring operating out of the Mahoney Resort on Waiheke Island in the Hauraki Gulf. I want you to check it out."

"And?" Jack's gut told him there was more to the story. The twitch of George's lips confirmed his suspicions.

"I've assigned you a partner."

Jack straightened from his casual sprawl against the wall, his eyes narrowing on his middle-aged boss. "I work alone. I don't work with a partner." His last one had died. Horribly. And he lived with that guilt. He wasn't damn well repeating the hellish experience.

"You can't do this job alone."

"Why not?" Jack demanded. "I've managed every other assignment on my own."

George leaned back in his chair, steepling his fingers and looking over the top in a thoughtful manner. While he appeared relaxed, Jack knew George would give him a tough battle should they ever decide to go the physical route during a disagreement. "This one might be a little difficult. Reuben J. Mahoney is a slippery character." The chair squeaked a protest each time the big man shifted his weight.

"I can handle anything he throws at me."

George glanced at the calendar pinned on the wall then cast his attention back to Jack. "There's a blue moon coming up. It might fall prior to the end of the case."

Jack filled in the blanks. The blue moon would erode his powers and make it difficult to retain his human form. Without constant sexual stimulation, he'd shift into a taniwha, the legendary dragon from Māori mythology. Jack snorted at the thought of being trapped in taniwha form in the middle of a mission. It had happened to other shifters on George Taniwha's staff but not to him. He imagined the pandemonium if he transformed in the middle of the bustling resort. A disdainful snort emerged.

Little did New Zealanders know, but the species taniwha survived and lived among them. Jack didn't intend to be the first taniwha to make headlines in the *New Zealand Herald*. No way. No how. If he had to find a woman to keep the monster at bay, then that was what he'd do.

"Okay," he conceded. "I guess a partner might help. Who's available? Hone? Billy?"

George issued a choking sound, merriment dancing across his lined face as he stuck his big-booted feet on his desk.

"What's so goddamn amusing?" Jack ground out.

Another chortle exploded from George.

Jack paced the length of the room, trying to combat the thrum of agitation working through his system. He paused to stare out the window, his mind taking in the yachts that zigzagged across the blue waters of Auckland Harbor. Finally, he turned away and stalked back to drop into the chair opposite George. He kept his expression neutral despite the amusement still simmering across his boss's face. "Let me in on the joke."

"You can partner up with Hone or Billy if you want, but

you might want to consider the special circumstances."

"What circumstances?" Hell, he had a hot date with Melissa tonight. Good, sweaty, no-strings sex. He didn't have time for this crap. "Either Hone or Billy. I'm not fussy."

"Reuben J. Mahoney runs a couples' resort. I'm assigning you a female partner."

"A female— *No*."

"I guess you can take Hone. Or Billy," George mused. "Of course, you'd have to share a room. And a bed." He shook his grizzled head. "Two taniwha in the same space. Add in a blue moon and things might get a mite ugly."

*Fuck*. Jack sent a hard glare at his boss. Trapped as neat as an eel in a net. Jack shuffled through the range of possibilities and came up blank. "Who is she?"

"A new operative."

Great. *Just bloody great*. Not only was he forced to take a female partner, he was getting a raw beginner. Jack didn't trust himself to speak so he firmed his mouth, folded his arms across his chest and scowled his displeasure.

"I'm teaming you with Emma Montrose."

"Your secretary?" Jack heard disbelief in his voice but thought he managed to keep his panic to himself. What the hell did a secretary know about investigating a case? What about the danger? To both of them. They would have to share a room, for God's sake. Jack refused to let his mind dwell on Emma's sexy legs...or the rest of her curvy form.

"Emma's capable of assisting you on this case."

"Assign me another case." Spending time alone with Emma was enough to give any hot-blooded male ideas. Jack wasn't interested in anything but sex. No relationships for him. Been there. Done that. Chucked away the T-shirt.

Nope. It was best he kept well away from the very curvy, brown-haired Emma Montrose. Every time he came into the office, her big blue eyes trailed after him like a pet dog expecting a treat, except instinct told him she had more in mind than stroking or petting. That was part of what caused his edginess whenever he was in her presence. A woman of Emma's caliber craved happily-ever-after.

Not his goal. Not anymore.

Some of the taniwha shifters—George, for example—were happily married, but finding a woman comfortable with her man turning into a dragon wasn't easy. It was a rare female who coped with the idea that her children might carry the taniwha gene. Or might not, depending on fate. The peculiarities of the taniwha species had rattled his ex-lover. She hadn't been able to cope with his *ugly appearance* and had run despite his assurances she would always remain human. He hadn't even reached the part about taniwha living longer—around thirty years longer—than the average human before his lover had run. Too late to tell her the benefit would extend to her.

"Did you say share a room?" Jack ignored the interested twitch from his cock.

"And a bed. But if you don't think you can act as part of a couple with Emma, I'll send Hone. He's due off assignment tomorrow."

Jack considered that for all of two seconds. He'd seen the way Hone looked at Emma. "I'll do it," he said, even though deep in his gut, he knew he'd regret this decision. "Give me the details."

THE NEXT MORNING, EMMA marched into the offices of George Taniwha Investigators and Security, a woman on a mission. After spending her twenty-fifth birthday with her girlfriends and not one suitable male candidate in sight, she'd made a resolution. With the help of her tipsy friends, she'd decided to go for broke.

Get Jack Sullivan to notice her or bust.

A smile—was that too much to ask? No, dammit, it wasn't, and that would be just the start. She intended to progress from there—from a smile and good morning to down-and-dirty sex. Her breasts tingled at the thought and a swooping sensation spiraled to her lower belly. Of course, she wouldn't go as far as stalking, but she wasn't going to act the shy little wallflower either.

Emma Montrose was coming out of the shade and going after the man she wanted. She intended to channel the fictional taniwha on George Taniwha Investigators and Security's letterhead—formidable and determined, ready to scare Jack into thinking her way. By the time she was finished, he'd know of her interest. Then, he could take the next step.

She drew herself up.

*No.* That wasn't right.

She refused to let him slide from her sights without a fight. She'd take the second step and as many other steps as the situation required.

Emma pushed aside several possible scenarios, concentrating on and visualizing the one she wanted. A secret smile curled across her lips as she fluffed her short curly hair.

Two lovers.

Emma and Jack.

Horizontal dancing.

Heat seeped into her cheeks. Emma yanked out her office wheelie chair, plonked down her butt and grabbed up a pile of envelopes off the desk to fan her face. This brave new Emma might embarrass her a little, but she'd try to keep up.

The front door of the office opened, and she straightened abruptly, her spine hitting the back of the chair. *Well.* No time like the present to put her plan into action.

Emma put her best receptionist manner into practice and flashed a smile. "Good morning, Jack."

The man froze in a possum-in-headlights pose, giving Emma the opportunity to look her fill. He was tall and built with a rower's powerful shoulders, slim hips and a butt that her fingers itched to grope. His hair was shiny black, halfway between short and long and in need of a cut, making her fingers itch to smooth the messy strands away from his face. A dreamy sigh squeezed past her lips. Blessed with sun-kissed skin, no matter what the season, she often fantasized about his appearance beneath the layers of clothing. Did the gorgeous olive tones—a legacy from his Māori ancestors—extend all over his body? Hopefully she'd sit in a position of knowledge soon.

"Morning."

The word came out as a grunt, but it was an improvement on his usual silence or what she called the office furniture treatment. She forced away a surge of nerves and looked him straight in the eye. "Are you here to see George?"

"Yeah."

"Okay." Emma's breath caught, her lungs filling with his seductive scent—something that reminded her of the mystical Orient with hints of orange and patchouli and a healthy dose of masculine musk. She stared, and the act of holding his gaze propelled heat across her skin. A hot fiery surge of self-conscious emotion.

Dangerous.

Crazy.

A challenge to her goal.

She sucked in a deep breath and puffed it back out again. The sight of his gorgeous masculine attributes made a woman imagine skin-to-skin contact. That big, strong form moving against hers, thrusting deep into her pussy, callused hands fondling her breasts, fingers plucking at her nipples. A sensuous shiver swept her and arousal soaked her panties without warning.

She gulped and licked suddenly dry lips. All that from merely passing pleasantries. What would happen if they were naked? Together?

*Get a grip*, she thought sternly as her hormones danced a frenzied jitterbug. A cough cleared her throat. "I'll let him know you're here."

Hmmm. Not bad for the first time. She'd improve with the next meeting.

"I don't mind waiting."

Emma felt her eyes grow round. Huh? What was wrong with this picture?

Jack closed the distance between them and used his forefinger to tap her under the chin. Her heart stuttered in a mad gallop. She gasped, jerking from his touch in outright shock.

The door from the street burst open, and George bounded inside followed by his son, Hone. "Ah, you're here, Jack. I thought you might change your mind."

"No," Jack snapped, glaring at Hone.

Hone ignored Jack's scowl and sauntered across the office to stop beside Emma. "Hello, sweetheart." He hauled her from her chair and wrapped her in a breath-stealing bear hug.

"Put her down," Jack growled.

"But I haven't seen her for a week." Hone nuzzled her neck and Emma giggled. "She's my girl."

"Don't you have a case to solve?" Jack looked as if he wanted to punch his friend.

Not in the least perturbed by his buddy's bad temper, Hone parked his butt on the corner of her desk and flashed a sexy grin. Emma sighed as she peeked through lowered lashes at Jack's surly face. Why couldn't she fall for Hone instead of grumpy Jack? It was a mystery, all right. Although Hone made her smile and was easy on the eye, he didn't affect her heart rate in the slightest.

Not like Jack.

George shook his head. "Hone, I want you to check into a case that came in yesterday. Mrs. Denning has a thief she needs to flush out. Emma can give you the details. Jack, I want to go over a few details regarding the case we discussed yesterday." He strode toward his office but paused in the doorway. "Emma, I need to see you in my office once you're finished with Hone."

Bother. She'd hoped George might let her gain some practical experience with Mrs. Denning's case. Obviously not. She scowled and decided it was time to remind George of his promise.

Five minutes later, Emma knocked lightly on George's door and entered. She carried a pad and pen to take notes. Jack was sprawled in a chair near the window. He jumped to his feet on seeing her.

"Ah, good." George checked his watch then stood. "I have a golf date. I'll leave you in Jack's capable hands."

George's words echoed in her mind for long drawn-out seconds. She heard the click of the door as her boss departed but couldn't concentrate on anything except the concept of capable hands. A mental picture popped into her mind, aided by fertile imagination. Masculine hands cupping her naked breasts, fingers plucking her sensitive nipples.

*Oh, my.* She subsided into a chair in case her legs buckled. Without warning, her cotton blouse felt several sizes too small and her face glowed with enough heat to cook a batch of pikelets for morning tea. She fanned her cheeks vigorously with her notepad.

"Are you feeling all right?" Emma's head snapped up to find Jack's enigmatic gaze settled on her. "You'll be as useful as a war canoe without a warrior to paddle if you fall sick."

"What...what do you mean?" Emma thought she understood but wanted clarity and confirmation.

"George wants you to help me with my case."

Emma jumped to her feet and pumped her fist in the air. "Yes!" She did an impromptu jig before noticing his gaze on her bouncing breasts. Emma froze then dropped into her chair, striving to keep embarrassment from crawling across her face. She *must* work on maintaining her cool.

"Don't get too excited. You're along on a trial basis. You help out with the grunt work. Do what I say, when I say with no questions asked. Clear?"

"No problem." Emma restrained her celebratory grin and the urge to give him a cheeky salute. *Hot damn*. She was gonna be a private dick. "What's the case?"

"We're investigating the Mahoney Resort on Waiheke Island. We think there's a drug ring running out of the resort. Sports-enhancing drugs."

"Sounds great. Are we going for the day? When are we

going?" Emma was finding it difficult to sit still instead of dancing in celebration. Her first case and closer contact with Jack all in one hit. Life couldn't get much better.

Jack scowled, a fierce frown, no doubt in an attempt to burst her bubble of enthusiasm. "We're going for a week. You'll need to pack tonight since we leave for Waiheke tomorrow. Here's the file. Read the documents carefully and let me know if you have questions."

Emma nodded eagerly. Their hands brushed during the file transfer and a frisson of pleasure zapped down her arm. Surprised, she jerked away, almost dropping the info in her haste. "I'll read it," she promised, her gaze lowering to screen her reaction. Her stomach swooped and plunged as if she were attached to a bungee cord. Aware of the burgeoning silence and Jack's disapproval, she hurried into speech. "What time do we leave?"

"The ferry departs at ten tomorrow morning. I'll pick you up at nine-thirty."

"I live at—"

"I know your address. Don't be late."

Learn more about BLUE MOON DRAGON.
https://shelleymunro.com/books/blue-moon-dragon/

# ABOUT AUTHOR

USA Today bestselling author Shelley Munro lives in Auckland, the City of Sails, with her husband and a cheeky Jack Russell/mystery breed dog.

Typical New Zealanders, Shelley and her husband left home for their big OE soon after they married (translation of New Zealand speak - big overseas experience). A twelve-month-long adventure lengthened to six years of roaming the world. Enduring memories include being almost sat on by a mountain gorilla in Rwanda, lazing on white sandy beaches in India, whale watching in Alaska, searching for leprechauns in Ireland, and dealing with ghosts in an English pub.

While travel is still a big attraction, these days Shelley is most likely found in front of her computer following another love - that of writing stories of contemporary and paranormal romance and adventure. Other interests include watching rugby (strictly for research purposes), cycling, playing croquet and the ukelele, and curling up with an enjoyable book.

Visit Shelley at her Website
www.shelleymunro.com

Join Shelley's Newsletter
www.shelleymunro.com/newsletter

# ALSO BY SHELLEY

**Paranormal**

*Middlemarch Shifters*

My Scarlet Woman

My Younger Lover

My Peeping Tom

My Assassin

My Estranged Lover

My Feline Protector

My Determined Suitor

My Cat Burglar

My Stray Cat

My Second Chance

My Plan B
My Cat Nap
My Romantic Tangle
My Blue Lady
My Twin Trouble
My Precious Gift


***Middlemarch Gathering***
My Highland Mate
My Highland Fling


***Middlemarch Capture***
Snared by Saber
Favored by Felix
Lost with Leo
Spellbound with Sly
Journey with Joe
Star-Crossed with Scarlett

Ingram Content Group UK Ltd.
Milton Keynes UK
UKHW040825200323
418846UK00004B/449

9 781991 063205